"Look Here, N_____
Vixen . . .

I think it's time for us to start over or at least clear things up. We're going to be living in pretty close quarters, and we'll be forced to work together, if only for a while. The least we can do is be friends."

Jana, uncertain of what to make of this overture, turned towards him with questioning eyes. "But, of course . . ."

That was all she had a chance to say before his strong arms went around her and his lips came down to meet hers. She struggled with shock and fury, but her body betrayed her. There was no mistaking her immediate and powerful response. As his lips probed hers, she felt herself giving in to the insistent pleasure of it, and her blood raced through her veins like fire. . . .

SUZANNE MICHELLE

can't decide which she loves more—her husband or writing. She lives in Texas and often writes about the West, which she knows so well. When she's not busy writing, she can often be found with her nose in a book, because reading is another of her favourite activities.

Dear Reader,

SILHOUETTE DESIRE is an exciting new line of contemporary romances from Silhouette Books. During the past year, many Silhouette readers have written in telling us what other types of stories they'd like to read from Silhouette, and we've kept these comments and suggestions in mind in developing SILHOUETTE DESIRE.

DESIREs feature all of the elements you like to see in a romance, plus a more sensual, provocative story. So if you want to experience all the excitement, passion and joy of falling in love, then SILHOUETTE DESIRE is for you.

I hope you enjoy this book and all the wonderful stories to come from SILHOUETTE DESIRE. I'd appreciate any thoughts you'd like to share with us on new SILHOUETTE DESIRE, and I invite you to write to us at the address below:

Jane Nicholls
Silhouette Books
PO Box 177
Dunton Green
Sevenoaks
Kent
TN13 2YE

SUZANNE MICHELLE
Enchanted Desert

Silhouette Desire

Published by Silhouette Books

Copyright © 1982 by Suzanne Michelle

First printing 1983

British Library C.I.P.

Michelle, Suzanne
   Enchanted desert.—(Silhouette desire)
   I. Title
   813'.54[F]   PS3563.I/

   ISBN 0 340 33569 6

Printed and bound in Great Britain for
Hodder and Stoughton Paperbacks, a
division of Hodder and Stoughton Ltd.,
Mill Road, Dunton Green, Sevenoaks,
Kent (Editorial Office: 47 Bedford
Square, London, WC1 3DP) by
Richard Clay (The Chaucer Press) Ltd.,
Bungay, Suffolk

1

~∞∞∞∞∞∞∞∞∞∞~

adies and gentlemen, thank you for flying with us. We hope you enjoy your stay in New Mexico, the Land of Enchantment.''

At the sound of the stewardess's voice Jana unbuckled her seat belt and looked out the window straight into the fiery splendor of a glorious New Mexico sunset. Flipping her long honey-blond hair back over her slender shoulders, she tugged at the lapels of the blue knit jacket that matched her startling azure eyes and accentuated her slender yet voluptuous body. Her poise and self-confidence were apparent in the flattering attire she had chosen for this trip, and in spite of the fatigue she felt after many hours on the plane, she looked fresh and collected. The long trip from Boston would seem an arduous journey to many, but to Jana it was the beginning of an exciting new life in an exotic place.

Albuquerque was Jana's first stop in New Mexico. The incredible chain of events that had led her to this barren, austere desert—the death of an aunt she had never known existed, the inheritance of a business in which she had no expertise, and the upheaval of leaving her neatly ordered life at the bookstore in Boston—were almost too much for her to comprehend. It had all happened so fast that her head was still spinning.

She had been relieved when she learned that the famous artist Fletcher Logan would meet her at the airport, but she wondered what he would think of her, the new owner of the gallery that had made him famous. She smiled at her image of Fletcher Logan as a paint-spattered, bearded figure in sandals and blue jeans who would probably want only to be left alone to pursue his art. The meager information she had been able to glean about him only made her all the more curious. A sophisticated, cosmopolitan man by all reports, he was apparently very guarded about the details of his personal life.

Before leaving Boston she had done her best to prepare herself for this new occupation by reading a number of art books and magazines, but she was painfully aware that this last-minute cramming was no substitute for years of interest and experience. She wanted to appear strong and calm and she realized that she would have to draw on her years of experience as a professional retailer. Managing an art gallery couldn't be that different from bookselling.

Taking a deep breath in anticipation, Jana pulled her overstuffed carryall from under her seat and stood up.

She was glad she didn't have to make arrangements for the trip by car from Albuquerque to Santa Fe. She squared her shoulders resolutely beneath the heavy bag, picked up her small black purse and started down the aisle of the airplane. She had no idea how she would recognize Fletcher Logan, but she felt capable of handling the situation.

As she made her way down the steps of the plane across the tarmac and into the airport she was impressed by the vast expanse of a seemingly limitless horizon washed with brilliant shades of red and orange and purple—a landscape far removed from the gray skies of Boston. The cool, crisp autumn air and the rose-colored sunset left Jana feeling breathless with anticipation, and at that particular moment she was delighted to be in that lovely place.

Two short weeks ago she had been comfortably ensconced in the serene life she had made for herself in Boston. She had been the buyer for Madison Street Bookshop, one of Boston's oldest book shops with a reputation for elegant first editions and antiquarian books. She was surrounded by beautiful leather-bound volumes that were as familiar to her as old friends. The customers who came to the quiet shop were friendly and polite. Because she knew them by name and knew their preferences in books, she had acquired a large and faithful following.

The quiet intimacy of the shop and the interesting people who shopped there afforded Jana an opportunity she might never have otherwise had for a steady and varied social life. Though she lived alone in a tiny apartment only a few blocks from the shop, without the benefit of the family background usually considered so important, she never lacked for stimulating companionship. Her quiet wit and natural charm, coupled with her vast knowledge of literature and rare books, made her much sought after and she was never without invitations.

In particular, Gary Rice, the son of one of Boston's oldest families and a Harvard professor with discriminating taste who collected rare medieval books, had become more than an acquaintance. They had settled into a comfortable ritual of dinners and movies and trips to Boston's art museums and historic sites highlighted by weekends with his family at their country home in Connecticut. His attempts to increase their intimacy were beginning to occur more and more frequently, but Jana knew that she would always be unable to respond to him as anything more than a comfortable friend. As Gary's tentative hints of marriage had become more and more insistent, aided by subtle hints from his family, Jana had tried vainly to return to the ease of their earlier friendship. At twenty-six she knew that marriage meant more than companionship and she was reluctant to become a part of the strictly regimented social life of Boston's upper class. His increasingly passionate lovemaking during the weekends they spent alone together left her unaroused and, even worse, afraid of hurting his feelings.

Just as things were reaching an intolerable crisis point the letter that was to change her life arrived via special delivery. She was at home enjoying the quiet solitude of her day off. Dressed in jeans and a lime-green sweater, she stared in disbelief at the ivory vellum envelope with the name of a prestigious Boston law firm engraved on the back. Lawyers had no place in her orderly life except for the kindly old gentleman who had administered the meager trust fund left by her parents for her education and nothing in her sheltered experience prepared her for the challenges set forth in the letter.

Fearing the worst, Jana opened the envelope with trembling fingers.

Dear Miss Fleming,

In cooperation with the law firm of Bates, Jackson and Lewis of Santa Fe, New Mexico, we have undertaken the task of contacting you in relation to the estate of your late aunt, Lee Grayson. Miss Grayson's precipitate demise left us with little information as to your actual whereabouts, though her will made clear that you are her only living relative. Please call at our office at your earliest convenience so that we may arrange the quick and efficient disposition of her estate.

The letter was signed by Carter Bates, attorney-at-law.

Jana laughed with amazement at the sheer absurdity of the mistake. Certain that if she had had any remaining relatives she would at least have been apprised of their existence in her twenty-six years. Chuckling to herself with obvious relief, she decided to call the lawyer's office the first thing the next morning and clear up the blatant error in identity.

When she phoned the law office the following morning and gave her name to the receptionist she was put through to Mr. Bates immediately.

"My dear Jana. I cannot tell you how glad I am to hear from you." The courteous voice was that of a man old enough to be her father.

"But there must be some mistake," Jana said without a doubt in the world, her clear voice confident and convincing.

"Oh, no. There is no mistake. We are quite cautious. You are Jana Fleming and were born in Andover, Massachusetts, the only child of Thomas and Sarah Fleming. Your parents perished in an airplane crash on their way home from a medical convention. You are presently employed at the Madison Street Bookshop. You see, my dear, we do not make mistakes."

Jana was shocked. Her life had suddenly become an open book, and unnerved that this soft-spoken lawyer had the key to her past, she was momentarily apprehensive, a mood she quickly tried to banish. The unsettling telephone conversation ended with a much-subdued Jana agreeing to meet Mr. Bates for lunch that very day.

As she entered the elegant wood-paneled bar of the Oak Room for lunch Jana was glad about the understated elegance of her brown tweed suit. Though she recognized many of the diners she had no idea how to find Carter Bates until the solicitous maître d' arrived at her side.

"May I be of assistance?"

"Why, yes," she said, grateful for his speed and thoughtfulness. "I'm here to meet Mr. Bates. Carter Bates, the attorney," she said in a soft voice that nevertheless commanded respect. The man's coolly obsequious expression changed immediately to one of graciousness at the mention of Carter Bates.

"Of course. Mr. Bates has his usual table. This way please."

As she followed the sleek maître d' across the plush interior she felt comfortable in the familiar surroundings, though she was more and more convinced that this was all a misunderstanding.

As he observed her approach a tall, silver-haired, portly gentleman rose from a corner table and clasped her slender hand with both of his when she arrived.

"I'm Carter Bates. You must be Jana."

Determined to enjoy this lunch in spite of the peculiar circumstances, Jana relaxed as she sat down and sank into the softness of the burgundy velvet cushions of the banquette. Still puzzled by the misunderstanding, she hastened to explain herself to Mr. Bates.

"I realize that you've gone to a great deal of trouble to arrange this meeting, but I'm sure there must be some mistake. I can't possibly be the Jana Fleming you're looking for." She took a quick sip of water from the glass already on the table, giving him a chance to respond.

"But, my dear, of course you are. We have spared neither time nor expense in our investigation. Every family has its secrets and there are things you don't understand. Let's dispense with the details of ordering before I continue."

He patted her hand as he motioned for the waiter and ordered lunch of salmon mousse, endive salad, white Moselle and a dessert of chocolate pot de creme. As the waiter hurried away the kindly lawyer turned his attention to Jana, who was toying with the folds of her napkin, feeling almost as if she were enjoying this under false pretenses.

"You see, Jana, over the past fifteen years your aunt, Lee Grayson, has earned a reputation as one of our nation's foremost art dealers. Santa Fe, as you may or may not know, is a fairly exclusive environment for artists. And Lee Grayson was something of an anomaly in the community. Her great genius was in discovering new talent. With somewhat limited means she managed to amass a huge fortune due to her perspicacity as a patron of the arts and her uncanny business acumen."

"But I've never heard of Lee Grayson. My parents never mentioned her." Jana was genuinely bewildered by the story unfolding before her at a time when she had been pleased with the secure and settled future she envisioned for herself.

Lee Grayson, the attorney went on, had been her mother's older sister. At the age of eighteen Lee had fallen in love with an artist. Her parents, Jana's grandparents, disapproved of his bohemian ways. Envisioning a life of abject poverty and disillusionment for their firstborn, they forbade the young man to set foot in their home, thus forcing Lee to make a decision between their way of life and his.

Fleeing the rigid societal constraints of her early upbringing, Lee cast aside her inhibitions and her parents' dire warnings and embraced the glamorous freedom of the Southwest. Her name was never mentioned by them again and Jana's mother had acquiesced to their wishes and kept silent as well. The love affair had faded, but by then Lee had already established herself as a *savante* of the Santa Fe art world and the Lee Grayson Gallery soon became known for bringing avant-garde artists to the attention of the world.

Jana shook her head in disbelief at this astonishing story of romance, adventure and success.

"But I never dreamed . . . I could never have imagined . . ." Jana was gripped with fear. That such a bold legacy was hers was more than she dared believe.

"Lee's rise to fame has been largely associated with her discovery and patronage of an artist named Fletcher Logan, who seemed destined from the first to make his mark on the national art scene. No doubt your mother would have told you what little she knew of her sister had her own death not been so untimely. As it is, you're the only surviving relative who can carry on the fine tradition of Lee Grayson's contributions to the art world." Mr. Bates paused in his tale, waiting for Jana's response.

But Jana, enraptured as she was by this incredible story of art and love, was quick to realize its implications for her future and found herself speechless. What did any of this have to do with her?

As if sensing her confusion Mr. Bates continued. "For the past six months the gallery has been operating under its own momentum. Lee would allow no one but Fletcher Logan to help her manage it. The local artists have cooperated to see that the gallery and Lee's ideas live on. But the management of the gallery cannot continue in this fashion. Someone must assume responsibility. I could, of course, assume that you have no interest in a field in which you have no expertise. We could liquidate all of Lee's assets, which would result in a tidy financial benefit for you. However, since Lee's will specifically leaves the management of her affairs to you, I suggest that you go out to Santa Fe and observe the situation for yourself. Of course, all of your expenses will be paid for by the estate.''

Jana had been inspired by this tale of her adventuresome ancestor and felt that she had to meet this challenge. Turning to the lawyer with a wide smile, she said, "If I am who you think I am I have no choice."

Now here she was—two short weeks later—in the Albuquerque airport. The bravado of that moment when she sat in the luxurious safety of the Oak Room with Mr. Bates seemed more than a little foolish. Her excitement faded and her new environment seemed suddenly hostile as she realized that there was no one to meet her. The waiting room was empty.

Jana decided to search for her luggage. She knew that she could rent a car if she had to and find her way to Santa Fe, but she didn't relish the thought of a trip alone at night after a day of traveling. For a moment it was all she could do to restrain herself from bolting to the ticket counter and buying a return ticket to Boston and the security she had left behind.

She was walking down the corridor to the baggage counter when a tall and imposing man collided with her, causing her to drop her heavy carryall. She tried to regain her balance but tripped over the carryall at her feet.

She sagged against the wall for support and found herself gazing at the tips of a pair of brown suede desert boots. Slowly her gaze was drawn upward along the powerful frame of the man who had bumped into her, past tight-fitting gray cords and a gray cashmere V-neck pullover that revealed a mass of dark curly hair on his chest. Finally her eyes were drawn to his aristocratic face with its chiseled features and tumble of raven-black hair, and for one fleeting moment she looked deep into penetrating steel-gray eyes that made no pretense of apology.

Jana flushed, embarrassed that she couldn't take her eyes off this man who had her in such an awkward position. She was mesmerized by his silver eyes and felt as if he were seeing clearly some part of her that she herself had never seen before.

She tried without success to untangle herself from the warm and powerful grip of the stranger's strong suntanned hands on her fragile arms, pale by comparison.

"Why don't you watch where you're going?" In spite of her growing fatigue from the long trip she was surprised at the sharpness of her words.

Without releasing the grip he had on her the man calmly replied with supreme arrogance, "Well, if silly daydreamers don't have anything better to do than walk around airports in a daze they deserve to be run into—and no doubt will be quite often."

When he was sure that she had regained her balance he released his hold on her, slowly drawing his hands down the length of her arms. She tingled at his touch and, still stunned from the unexpected collision, heard the censure in his voice and felt angry as a result.

His powerful, probing eyes surveyed her slight form in appraisal as he towered over her like a giant, taking in every detail of her appearance. In a strained moment of silence he studied her with complete objectivity and Jana flushed beneath his scrutiny. For a moment she wished that she had worn a blouse with a less revealing neckline, for his gaze lingered at her throat and on the soft cleavage of her breasts.

Obviously pleased with what he saw, he softened his voice. "Since you're clearly unable to cope on your own I'll help you find your luggage. You'll never find the baggage counter by yourself." He brushed against her as he grabbed the carryall, and she was keenly aware that he didn't miss the soft curves of her trim legs.

"Having come hundreds of miles under my own power, I feel quite certain that I can manage on my own," Jana flung back at him recklessly, hoping that the tardy Fletcher Logan wouldn't pick this moment to arrive on the scene.

She was propelled along the corridor as though she had no say in the matter, her arm in the astonishingly powerful grip of this disturbing man who now had possession of the one bag, which contained the most important documents of her life. She was profoundly aware of his masculine strength and muscular physique, and his very closeness made her keenly aware of her own femininity.

When they reached the baggage counter Jana noticed with dismay that her bags were almost the only ones left on the carousel. She must have surrendered to her daydreams of her life in Boston and her meeting with Mr. Bates longer than she had realized. The stranger came to an abrupt halt, pulling her close to him when he stopped. With a jerk of his thumb in the direction of her luggage he said in an insufferably mocking voice that made no effort to hide a derisive pleasure in her discomfort, "Those must be yours."

Feeling that she was indeed a silly daydreamer after all, she could only nod in agreement. She felt that she had left her resolve for independence outside with the sunset. She once again looked around for Fletcher Logan and wondered what could have delayed him.

The stranger lifted her heavy luggage with no apparent effort, then turned to her and said in a clipped voice, "Well, where is he? No woman comes this far without a man to meet her."

Jana bridled at this, but realizing that he now had possession of all her luggage, she decided to answer him civilly. "I'm afraid I'm alone—by choice. Now, if you'll kindly show me the way to the car-rental counter you will have amply repaid me for your rudeness."

His eyes turned to ice and he seemed about to speak, but apparently thinking better of it, he shrugged carelessly and strode off in the direction of the car-rental counter, still carrying her luggage.

Still shaken from the fall, she had to run to keep up with his purposeful stride. She was more than a little afraid of him, but she couldn't help noticing the determined set of his handsome jaw as he turned away from her.

She was breathless when they reached the counter and he set down her luggage, but she was determined to rid herself of his disturbing companionship. Handsome though he was, his overbearing presence had gone on long enough. Tiny darts of alarm pierced her and she was acutely aware of her own vulnerability in this strange and unfamiliar place.

"I can manage from now on. Thank you for your trouble." At least now she had her luggage back.

Without a word he turned from her and vanished as quickly as he had appeared.

Still somewhat stunned by the encounter, Jana turned to find that no one was in attendance at the car-rental counter. The clerks had either gone to supper or were working in the back office. Indeed, the only sign of their existence was a small silver bell and a sign that said "Ring for Assistance." She decided to take advantage of the moment to collect her thoughts.

She was facing a challenging array of possibilities. She could rent a car, study the map and try to make her way into Santa Fe on her own. She could spend the night in a hotel in Albuquerque, but that would mean either taking a taxi or renting a car the next morning and Mr. Logan would have no way of finding her. She could call the Grayson Gallery, but it was well after business hours. The thought of waiting alone in the airport bar was not appealing to her. She was trying to choose the best course when she heard her name broadcast over the airport paging system.

"Will Jana Fleming please report to the information desk?" She was overcome with a mixture of relief and surprise. Awkwardly struggling with her luggage, she made her way down a flight of stairs following the arrows indicating the direction of the information desk. At the bottom of the stairs her heart lifted at the sight of the huge Information sign and then plummeted

18

downward as she recognized the tall figure standing there.

Exhausted from lugging her baggage down the long flight of stairs, she dropped her things and sat down on the large suitcase and met head on the incredulous stare of the stranger she had collided with just a few minutes earlier.

When she saw the look of exasperation on his face she put her hands over her mouth, holding back gales of hysterical giggles, completely oblivious to the astonishingly beautiful picture she made.

"We've got to stop meeting like this," she joked, her face flushed with pink and her long hair tousled in a casual manner that made her even more appealing.

"Miss Fleming, I presume?" he inquired with mock gallantry.

Laughing helplessly at the absurdity of it all, she said, "You can't be Fletcher Logan. You don't even look like an artist." She could tell by the look on his face that what she had said had come out wrong.

His whole body stiffened, and arching an eyebrow, he regarded her coldly for a moment. As he picked up her luggage he said, "You obviously haven't met many artists."

Sensing that she had wounded him in some inexplicable way, she surrendered meekly and said, "You're right. I haven't." She followed him out of the airport to his car, which was waiting in the lonely desert night.

2

꘎꘎꘎꘎꘎꘎꘎꘎꘎

The cool, crisp breeze, carrying with it the first hint of winter, caressed Jana's face. Tossing her head from side to side like a restless child who couldn't remember where she had gone to sleep, Jana finally woke herself up. Sitting upright in the strange bed, she blinked at the unfamiliar surroundings and finally pinched herself to make certain that this was reality and not a dream.

The soft bed creaked gently under her weight as she rose to walk to the open window. Looking out into the morning sunshine, she glimpsed the colorful central plaza where Indian merchants were already gathered to sell their wares—pottery, woven blankets, turquoise jewelry. Standing in the cool air in her pale pink velour dressing gown and shivering, Jana could sense the picturesque town of Santa Fe coming to life. Resolved not to let the day begin without her, she headed toward the shower to shake off her sleepiness and assume her role in the stirring town below her.

Under the stinging needles of the warm shower Jana washed away the weariness of the preceding day's journey. She recalled with embarrassment that she had fallen asleep almost immediately upon entering Fletcher Logan's car, completely missing the drive from Albuquerque to Santa Fe. She vaguely remembered his husky, masculine voice saying, "I think you've had enough new experiences for one day. Tony Phillips expects to begin working with you first thing in the morning. You can stay in town here at the La Fonda tonight and we'll drive out to the ranch tomorrow afternoon."

She remembered wondering at the time who Tony Phillips was and what he had to do with her, but she was too sleepy to ask any questions. It was all she could do to follow him into the La Fonda Hotel. Apparently he had made these arrangements in advance, for she couldn't recall checking in. Fletcher himself had carried her bags up to the room.

She had sunk into the nearest chair while he placed her bags on the luggage rack at the foot of the bed and put her overnight case in the bathroom. She must have dozed off, for the next thing she remembered she had been lying on the bed, moaning with sleepy pleasure as sensitive fingers caressed her tired neck and shoulders. She could feel someone gently unbuttoning her blouse and she knew that she should wake up, but she just couldn't. Not until she felt his hands rub across the bare skin above her bra.

"What do you think you're doing?" she demanded.

"I thought that might wake you up." Fletcher laughed in genuine amusement, scarcely taking his eyes off her unbuttoned blouse and ample, curvaceous breasts.

Pushing him away, Jana had wrenched herself free of his grasp and struggled to her feet, clutching the open front of her blouse. "I can undress myself, thank you. But I'll wait until you leave, if you don't mind."

"Not a bit," Fletcher replied with mocking good humor. "I knew you weren't that kind of girl. And I'm in no hurry, because I'll be seeing a lot more of you. I like what I've seen so far."

Before she had time to wonder what he meant by that last remark he had shut the door behind him. She had bolted the chain lock on the door and fallen into bed after what seemed an endless search for her warmest nightgown. As she had drifted off to sleep she couldn't help remembering the gentleness of his strong hands and the deep timbre of his voice.

Blushing at the memory of the night before, Jana knew that she must put all this behind her and keep her relationship with Fletcher on a purely business level. As she stepped out of the tub she wrapped herself in a large, fleecy towel. Then she gazed into the bathroom mirror and noted with satisfaction that sleep had erased the dark circles under her eyes. After brushing her silky blond hair back over her shoulders in its casual flip style she leaned forward to apply her rudimentary makeup—a touch of blusher, lipstick and eye shadow completed her toilet—and she smiled with pleasure at the face peering back at her from the mirror.

She emerged from the bathroom feeling renewed and refreshed, then examined the contents of her suitcase, trying to find the perfect outfit for the first day of her new life. Out of habit, as if she was dressing for a typical fall day at the bookstore, she reached for a pair of beige wool slacks, a fawn silk blouse, a tailored navy blazer and brown suede boots. She caught a glimpse of herself in the mirror; she looked composed and competent and the thought gave her confidence.

She was considering going down to breakfast when the phone rang. She hurried to answer it, assuming that only Fletcher Logan knew where she was. In spite of herself, she looked forward to talking to him.

"Good morning," Jana said cheerfully.

"Hello," said a strange voice—definitely not Fletcher Logan's. Jana would have known that voice anywhere. "This is Tony Phillips."

"Tony who?" she asked, momentarily puzzled.

"Tony Phillips. I realize we haven't met, but nevertheless I have anticipated your arrival with great interest. I thought we might get started first thing this morning."

Her confusion increased. "I'm sorry, Mr. Phillips, but I haven't the slightest idea who you are. Am I supposed to know you?"

"But I thought surely Fletcher would have explained. . . ."

"I'm afraid Mr. Logan didn't explain much of anything to me." Jana could feel her face redden at the thought of her last encounter with Fletcher.

"Well, since he's the one who told me how to reach you I thought surely you would be expecting my call. I didn't mean to disturb you so early in the morning, but I thought you might like to start working as soon as possible. Since I'm the bookkeeper for the gallery I thought going over the books with you would be the logical way to start."

"Oh, of course," Jana said, remembering with sudden clarity that Fletcher had mentioned someone by that name.

"Have you had breakfast yet? I hoped perhaps I could join you for a cup of coffee. I look forward to showing you around Santa Fe and introducing you to Grayson Gallery."

"That would be lovely; I was just walking out the door when you called." Jana found herself looking forward to meeting this pleasant-sounding man and getting her first day at the gallery under way.

"Great. Why don't we meet downstairs in the La Fonda restaurant in fifteen minutes?"

Before leaving her room Jana took one last look at herself in the mirror. At least she looked the part of a respectable businesswoman, no matter how unsure she felt inside.

Descending the steps to the restaurant, she ran her fingers down the ornate carved wood of the banister and realized that she would have to become accustomed not only to being the owner of a famous art gallery but also to being the heiress of the legacy of Santa Fe's most prominent citizen. Despite being self-conscious in her strange surroundings, she knew she must not let her unknown aunt down.

The headwaiter showed her to a corner table in the bright, sunny room lush with greenery and, in the center, a bubbling fountain. As she contemplated the menu with its strange Mexican dishes she marveled at the exotic surroundings—the Mexican-tiled floor, the spilling fountain, the tanned waiters and waitresses. After her first cup of coffee she ordered, with false bravado, a dish of scrambled eggs and green chiles, with flour tortillas on the side.

She was pleasantly surprised to find that the strange food was very much to her liking. Leaning back in the Mexican wooden chair, she contemplated her second cup of coffee. Everyone in the room looked so casual, yet so elegant—she began to worry that she looked too much the proper Bostonian in her business clothes. She could see that she'd need a new wardrobe in order to fit in here.

She was roused from her daydream by the approach of a nice-looking young man of about her own age. His blond hair was cut short and he wore large tortoise-shell glasses that accentuated the serious look on his face. He shook hands with her as he introduced himself.

"Jana Fleming?" In response to her smiling nod he broke into a boyish grin that seemed appropriate with his faded jeans and western-cut gingham shirt. "I'm Tony Phillips. It's good to meet you at last." He took off his denim sports jacket, hanging it over the back of his chair as he joined Jana at the table.

"And you, too," she said, hoping she sounded calm and professional. "I'm sure we have a lot to go over together. There's so much for me to learn."

Half an hour later Jana's head was swimming with facts and figures. She had taken pages of notes and the tabletop was covered with papers—profit-and-loss statements, balance sheets, lists of names and addresses. She looked up to see an elegant, sophisticated woman standing beside Tony, gold bracelets dangling on her arm as she rested it on his shoulder.

"How are things at Grayson Gallery these days, Tony? Do you think they're ready to sell out? You know I've always wanted an art gallery of my very own." Her sleek black hair fell to her shoulders, as shiny as the gold loop earrings she wore. The tall, willowy woman smiled and her green, teasing eyes sparkled, but nothing could hide her serious intent.

Tony turned in his chair and disengaged himself from her overly familiar embrace. "As a matter of fact, Taylor, things are improving even as we speak. You're just in time to meet the new owner, Jana Fleming. Jana, this is Taylor Randall. She's one of Fletcher's greatest admirers."

Jana reached across the table to shake Taylor's outstretched hand. The other woman's long, lacquered nails were immaculate and she flashed an emerald ring set in a circle of diamonds. Jana inwardly recoiled at the woman's insinuating manner, but she had already learned from her discussion with Tony that Taylor Randall was one of the gallery's most generous financial supporters. She had to swallow her initial impulse to dislike the irritating, self-composed woman. Gallery business must come first.

"Won't you join us for a cup of coffee?" Jana tried hard to make her voice welcoming and pleasant.

Taylor smoothed back her straight black hair and looked at Jana through narrowly appraising eyes. She wore lavender velvet designer jeans and a matching silk shirt. Around her tiny waist she wore a thin leather belt clasped with an ivory snake head.

"So you're the new kid in town. Breaking into the art scene in Santa Fe is tougher than you might suppose. But if you think you can do it, more power to you." Taylor smiled sweetly at Jana.

Jana drew back as if stung. "Thanks, but I think my aunt has already done that for me." Jana's voice was calm, but inwardly she was shaken and angry.

As if Jana hadn't spoken, Taylor continued speculatively, "I wonder how you and Fletcher will get along. I adore him myself, but he eats little girls like you for breakfast. Maybe I'd better put in a good word for you when he comes over for our morning coffee." Taylor's smile was almost too sweet as she turned to Tony and said, "I think I'll pass on that cup of coffee for now, Tony. I have things to do." Taylor wished him a good day and gracefully made her way across the room. Jana could tell by the way Taylor walked that she was conscious of the many eyes that followed her progress.

Tony turned to Jana with admiration in his hazel eyes. "Well, you certainly handled that well." He explained that Taylor was the daughter of one of Santa Fe's first families. She had been educated in exclusive private schools in the East and studied art at the Sorbonne in Paris. She was on the board of the Santa Fe Opera, had an apartment in New York City and a home in Santa Fe.

"Taylor is a major collector. She's bought up a lot of Fletcher's work, and for reasons I don't quite understand, Lee always seemed quite fond of her." Tony finished his coffee.

"But is she serious about buying the gallery?" Jana hoped that Tony would brush that suggestion aside as a joke. She didn't relish the idea.

"There was a very real possibility of that when we thought we couldn't find you. But now that you're here there's no threat of that."

Jana nodded, but something told her he wasn't as confident as he sounded. Wanting to understand all the ramifications of her new position, she asked the question that had been nagging at her since her arrival in Santa Fe. "Tony, why didn't Lee Grayson leave the gallery to Fletcher?"

"That's what we all assumed would happen. But no one knew until the will was read that Lee had any living relatives." Tony signaled to the waiter for the check.

Jana sensed that Tony was avoiding answering her question. It was obviously something he didn't want to discuss. She began to suspect that Fletcher Logan must have been sorely disappointed to learn of her existence.

As if reading Jana's mind Tony added, "I can see that this will take some getting used to, Jana, but I really think that the best thing to do is get started right away. And don't underestimate yourself—you have all the basic business skills down pat. It's just a matter of applying them to art instead of books. Come on. Let's head over to the gallery."

Strolling out into the bright Santa Fe sunshine, Jana was overwhelmed by the serene beauty of the scene.

When she had arrived late the previous night she had been so tired that she hadn't really taken it all in. Now, in the morning light, she found herself charmed by the quaint plaza. Indian craftsmen were already stationed in front of the Governor's Palace, ready with displays of native pottery and the almost ubiquitous turquoise and silver jewelry.

As they walked across the plaza Tony pointed out some of the local sights and characters. Leading her down San Francisco Street, he stopped in front of an attractive glass storefront in a small adobe shopping center.

"Here we are. This, I hope, is going to be a happy part of your new life—Grayson Gallery."

Tony presented the keys to Jana with a little flourish. She unlocked the door eagerly, curious to see what awaited her within. With a brave smile she walked into the cool, dark interior.

Following her, Tony reached for a switch and threw the room into dazzling light. Jana was stunned; everywhere she looked she saw beautiful things—the finest Indian pottery, Navajo blankets and exquisite paintings.

"I can see that this is truly the very best of everything. No wonder my aunt loved it so!"

"Yes, she did. This gallery was her whole life—I know she would have loved to be here to share it with you."

"I wish she were," Jana said with real regret. "I wish I had known her."

The two of them spent the rest of the morning going over the gallery's inventory. The time passed quickly

—so quickly that Jana felt she might have been in a dream. At noon Tony went out for sandwiches, leaving Jana alone for a few minutes. She found herself wandering through the gallery, lost in contemplation, amazed at the dazzling array of art that her aunt had collected.

And it was all arranged so beautifully! Jana felt as if she had wandered into someone's home, a home furnished with exquisite taste and style. She was losing her heart to the gallery, and she knew it. Even if it hadn't been her aunt's, even if she had only walked in by chance, she would have fallen in love with it in much the same way.

She thought of Fletcher Logan and wondered if he too loved the gallery. No doubt he did—what artist wouldn't?—and so much of his career, his hopes and dreams, must be tied up in these rooms. She puzzled again over what he must think of her—a young upstart with no training appearing at the doorstep as the new owner.

Moving from painting to sculpture to painting, trying to memorize the various works, she was startled by a deep, masculine voice. "See anything you like?"

Whirling about so that she almost lost her balance, Jana found herself looking right into dark, penetrating eyes that scrutinized her every move, her every thought.

"You!" she sputtered. She was drawn to his strong magnetic presence, but drew back instinctively, re-membering his high-handed arrogance of the night before.

"Yes, me," he answered with that calm, masculine

assurance she had already found so infuriating. "I told you I'd be seeing you again. I see you have no difficulty with buttons after all." His eyes followed the tiny pearl buttons of her silk blouse and she blushed at the memory of his sensual hands caressing her soft skin.

Jana felt very vulnerable, alone in the gallery with this man who towered over her. She didn't trust her own emotions and hoped fervently that he couldn't sense her strong and immediate response. They were interrupted by the sound of Tony's voice as he entered the front door of the gallery. Fletcher laughed as Jana stepped guiltily away from him.

"Well, Jana, I hope you'll be happy with the lunch I've found. It'll have to do." Tony had bought ham-and-cheese sandwiches and seemed oblivious to the tension in the room.

The three made polite small talk while Jana and Tony ate. After the luncheon debris had been disposed of Tony rose and glanced at his watch. "Do you feel like taking a ride out to the ranch, Jana?"

Before Jana could reply, Fletcher spoke up with authority. "I'll take her, Tony. I can show Jana over the place as well as anyone. Besides, I'm about ready to drive home anyway and it would save you the trip."

Despite the desperate look that Jana cast in his direction Tony acquiesced in his usual mild manner. "I'd appreciate it, Fletcher. That would give me time to settle a few other things this afternoon."

The three of them locked up the gallery and walked back across the square to the hotel.

"This is where I leave you, Jana," Tony said.

"Fletcher can set you up with Lee's car once you're out at the ranch so you won't feel totally cut off. I'll plan on meeting you at the gallery first thing in the morning—say ten o'clock?"

Jana nodded, shook his hand, then turned to enter the hotel, all the while shaking with silent fury. The very idea of being turned over to Fletcher irritated her, in spite of the fact that she was undoubtedly attracted to him. If only he weren't so sure of himself. Though she did so reluctantly, she could easily imagine Fletcher having his morning coffee with the beautiful and rich Taylor Randall. The two were most certainly cut out for each other.

The thought of Taylor and Fletcher as a couple made Jana more determined than ever to learn enough about the gallery to gain Fletcher's respect. It had not yet occurred to her that she might compete with Taylor as a woman, but she was certain that she could meet her on her own ground professionally.

Fletcher followed Jana into the hotel lobby and then, to her discomfort, continued with her up the stairs to her room.

"If you'll wait downstairs," she said, "I'll only take a minute to pack."

"Not a chance," he said, taking her arm proprietarily. "I know how you women are. If I sit down here and wait you'll take forever. And we need to stop and pick up a few provisions before we make that long trek out to the ranch. I'll just come with you and make sure that you get everything. We'll be on the road before you know it."

Jana was uncomfortably aware of his firm hand on

her arm. Her flesh burned with his very touch. Just being near him made her dizzy with feelings too complicated to sort through. Jana was puzzled that she could be attracted to a man whom she also found so infuriating.

She entered the room quickly, pulling free of him as she did so. He followed her as she headed for the bathroom to gather up the perfume and cosmetics she had left there. Although she tried not to be, she was uncomfortably aware of his solid and disturbing form filling the small doorway.

Meeting her eyes in the mirror, he spoke in an unexpectedly quiet voice. "Look here, my little vixen, I think it's time for us to start over, or at least clear things up. We're going to be living in pretty close quarters and I'm afraid we'll be forced to work together, if only for a while—and that, of course, is your choice. The least we can do is be friends."

Jana, uncertain of what to make of this overture, turned toward him with questioning eyes. "But, of course . . ."

That was all she had a chance to say before his strong arms went around her and his lips came down to meet hers. She struggled a bit with shock and fury, but her body betrayed her. No matter what she thought she felt intellectually, there was no mistaking her immediate and powerful response to this man. As his lips probed hers she felt herself giving in to the insistent pleasure of the kiss and her blood raced through her veins like fire. Her fists ceased their futile beating against his chest and her arms, almost of their own volition, reached up across his broad chest to twine themselves around his neck. As the pressure of his kiss increased Jana found herself ready to melt into the pure passion and emotion of it, but with a tremendous effort she brought herself back to reality.

"No!" she exploded, but her voice didn't quite have the strength she had hoped it would.

"That's a funny way of saying no," Fletcher drawled, looking at her appraisingly. "Your voice may be saying no, but the rest of that pretty little body of yours is saying yes, yes, yes."

"That's what you think," Jana said, her anger quite real now. "Do you make a habit of accosting women in their bathrooms?"

"No," he said airily, dismissing her inference. "Once we get to the ranch I think I'll make a habit of accosting you, as you put it, in the kitchen. We do share a kitchen, or didn't you know?"

"What do you mean?" Jana demanded.

"Didn't Tony tell you?" Fletcher was enjoying every minute of her obvious discomfort.

"Tell me what?"

"That I'll be living at the ranch with you. Don't worry; the kitchen is the only thing we share. My studio and living quarters are attached to the main house. They're quite sufficient; all it lacks is a kitchen."

This was the last straw for Jana. She turned her back to him without another word and finished packing her vanity case, then pushed past him and entered the bedroom, flinging things into her suitcases. She wasn't going to give him the satisfaction of favoring him with another word.

Five minutes later they were standing in the hotel lobby with Fletcher giving the desk clerk instructions on how to handle her room charges, drowning out Jana's efforts to speak for herself.

Fletcher shouldered Jana's bag without so much as a glance in her direction and strode out to the curb, where a handsome brown-toned pickup truck was parked. He tossed her cases into the truck and went around to the driver's side, not even bothering to open Jana's door for her. She stood there on the curb for a moment as he climbed into his seat, and for a brief instant she toyed with the idea of turning around and walking right back into the La Fonda. But then she realized how impossible that would be. I guess he comes with the territory, she told herself.

She opened the door of the truck and climbed in. After slamming the door behind her she looked straight ahead, feigning indifference as Fletcher started the car and began to drive around the plaza, heading out to the highway which led out of Santa Fe.

When they stopped at a grocery store Jana accompanied him inside with little grace, watching him narrowly as he picked out the necessary provisions. There was an awkward moment at the checkout stand when she wondered if she would be expected to pay, but Fletcher neatly solved the problem for her by telling the cashier to put it on his account; then, carrying all the bags himself, he strode out to the truck and loaded the groceries in the back.

When they stopped at a small adobe liquor store she turned to him with raised eyebrows.

"Can I get anything here for you?" he asked as he opened the door.

"Perhaps some white wine or some sherry," she said diffidently. "I'll wait here."

"Right," he said grimly, returning a few minutes later with a brown paper bag filled with bottles which he carefully balanced on the seat between them.

The uneasy silence between them continued as Fletcher turned the powerful truck onto the highway leading into the desert. Jana was surprised by how late it had become and she was astounded to notice the first spectacular signs of one of Santa Fe's fabled sunsets spreading across the sky. Any anger or indignation she might have felt quickly evaporated in the face of the magnificence before her. It seemed as if nature were playing with her palette, bringing out a dazzling array of colors to splash upon the sky. Purple, pink, mauve, gold, a brilliant orange—Jana felt sure that she had never experienced anything like the sheer beauty of this sunset before. Looking over at Fletcher, she noticed that the muscles in his face had relaxed and that he too seemed to be enjoying the show.

"I've never seen anything like this," she ventured softly, wanting him to know that she noticed and appreciated the beauty of her new surroundings.

"And you never will again," he said almost brusquely. "Each sunset is special and unique. The thrill never leaves you. When you find the sunsets boring, that's when it's time to leave Santa Fe. That's why the artists come to New Mexico. It's the light. There's nothing like it on earth."

The tension between them had vanished for the moment and Jana decided to sit back and enjoy the trip. As the glorious sunset began to fade she noticed that they had gone miles along the highway and Fletcher was already slowing the truck to turn into a desert road, though it seemed little more than a trail, actually.

"Where are we?" she asked, wondering how she would ever find her way back to Santa Fe on her own. She had paid little attention to the route they had been following.

"We're almost home," he replied calmly and Jana heard his words with both a thrill of delight and a slight shiver of alarm. How would she handle this new situation? And would they really be living in each other's pockets, as Fletcher has suggested? Remembering the warmth of his lips on hers, she cast a glance at him from beneath her long lashes and felt a tingle of anticipation. Blushing at her thought, she turned her attention to the road ahead. The truck rounded the last turn and came to a stop in front of an impressive adobe compound.

"Is *this* the ranch?" Jana said with surprise in her voice. She had been expecting something rather primitive and rustic, not this elegant simplicity.

The compound stood high on a hill with a breathtaking view of the valley below. The simple adobe architecture was of the desert, but yet not of it, an organic blend of landscape and dwelling place. Mesquite and cactus provided green touches here and there on the hill. No one had ever told Jana that the desert would be so green—or so beautiful.

She wondered if she would ever be able to look at Boston in the same way. Already she feared she was losing her heart to New Mexico.

She had been so lost in her admiration of the view that she had failed to notice that Fletcher had let himself out of the truck and had come around to her side and was now standing with the door open, waiting to help her out. Looking at her face, he laughed with genuine appreciation.

"Yes, Jana, this is home. And it looks like you're here to stay." The last rays of the sunset were fading as they unloaded the truck and carried the heavy bags of groceries into the house, an easy camaraderie existing between them for the first time.

3

Jana's admiration of the La Fonda Hotel had left her quite unprepared for the architecture of Lee Grayson's house. This was the real thing—and it was beautiful. The gently sloping adobe walls faced a small courtyard that was landscaped with beautiful desert flora and elegant stone sculpture. Jana hung her jacket on an attractive brass coatrack and ventured into the living room to the left of the entry. The living room was stunning—a living space that conveyed the strong message that someone had really *lived* and worked and possibly even loved here.

A grand piano dominated the center of the space. Every wall was filled with polished oak bookshelves, which gave the room a cozy air, and Jana noticed the extensive collection of art books—everything from big glossy picture books to small monographs and catalogues. What a library! Everything in the room seemed to gravitate toward the *hogar,* the gently rounded corner fireplace common to many houses in New Mexico. Jana had seen only a few of these fireplaces, primarily in photographs, and for the first time she began to understand how the hearth could be the center of the home. She was so lost in admiration that she didn't even hear Fletcher come into the room and deposit her suitcases right behind her.

"Remember me?" he asked, laughing at the expression on her face. "You seemed to be in another world."

"I think I was," she admitted, surprised into total honesty. "But I think I liked it."

"Well, good," he said in husky masculine tones, a slightly puzzled look on his face. "Then let's explore some more of it."

A gently curving arch led to a long narrow dining room, in the center of which was a gleaming mahogany table. The walls of the dining room were white and bare of furniture. The only adornments were the gorgeous paintings—all views of the desert at sunset. There were four of them, one on each wall, and Jana admired them for a long time in silence, quite unaware that Fletcher was observing her intently.

"They're magnificent," she said finally, turning to him with shining eyes. "And they're yours, aren't they?"

"Why, yes," he said, looking at her with some surprise, "but how did you know?"

"Oh, I knew," she said with more confidence than she felt. "I'm not totally ignorant, you know. And

So Wicked My Desire
— Stephanie Blake

A Companion in Joy R
— Dorothy Mack   602

Midnight Surrender 603
— Margaret Major Cleaves

Black Prince x   2385
— Elizabeth R. Hankin

Julie's Girl* — Vivian
2389   Donald

besides, there was something you said about the sunset. . . ." Her voice trailed off in a teasing manner.

Fletcher drew back and looked at her appraisingly. "For a Yankee," he drawled in bored southwestern tones, "you're certainly full of surprises."

She blushed, thinking that perhaps she had somehow betrayed her thoughts, and decided to be a little more businesslike. After all, the two of them were going to be working together in the gallery. It would never do to get too involved—if she weren't too involved already.

A narrow hall led off the dining room to what Jana thought must certainly be the most wonderful kitchen in the world. Gleaming copper pans and a profusion of baskets hung from the ceiling above a central cooking island. Two walls of the kitchen held ceiling-to-floor windows, one set looking out on the central courtyard Jana had spotted from the entryway. The others faced out on a long narrow sunroom, which itself had a sweeping view of the valley below. Jana looked over all the culinary accessories on the counter, ranging from a food processor to a coffee grinder, gleaming gadgets with dials and blades that all looked quite intimidating.

She looked around in dismay. "All this looks quite professional," she said, hating to admit her unfamiliarity with the kitchen. "In Boston I only had a small apartment with a minuscule kitchen; I'm not sure all this is quite necessary."

"Oh, it is," Fletcher responded with a confident laugh. "It's just that you haven't met Maria yet."

Jana groaned inwardly. Not another surprise! "And who might Maria be?"

"Why, our—or rather *your*—cook," Fletcher shot back. "Lee's had her for years—and spoiled her, too. That's not to say that she hasn't spoiled us as well. Wait until you taste her margaritas and *nachos*. You'll think you've died and gone to heaven."

Jana was relieved. At least their shared domesticity didn't include preparing meals together. She had never heard of sharing a kitchen in quite this way before. She felt a very long way from Boston.

Once again, as if sensing her thoughts, Fletcher laughed. "I may be an ogre across the breakfast table, but at least you don't have to prepare my *huevos rancheros!*"

Had she really been that transparent? Jana had to laugh with him. "I wouldn't have the first idea how to prepare them. I'm afraid I'm not much of a cook myself."

"Oh, you will be," Fletcher shot back with confidence. "With a setup like this, who could resist the chance to at least experiment?"

"You might be right."

Fletcher was reaching into the capacious refrigerator and pulling out a bottle of champagne. He proffered it in her direction. "Come on, the least we can do is celebrate your arrival in your new home!"

Minutes later the two were chatting away in easy camaraderie as they drank the champagne out of elegant fluted crystal glasses and put away the groceries. Fletcher pulled out an enormous platter of sandwiches that Maria had left in the refrigerator and they carried the food and champagne out into the narrow little sun room to eat and, as Fletcher said, "to catch the last of the light."

The sun room was simple yet elegant, like the rest of the house. The white adobe walls were hung with woven Navajo blankets and the furniture was comfortable, if a trifle worn, leather. A long low table held the food, its former burden of magazines having been hastily pushed aside to make room for their dinner. A picnic atmosphere prevailed. They ate and sipped champagne and watched the night come down around them.

Jana had never seen such a dramatic nightfall. Like the sunset, it was fantastic. Every imaginable shade of blue and purple was offered up by the sky and the mountains for their enjoyment, from the most delicate mauve to the deepest royal blue. Jana, enchanted, fell silent. Only after moments of rapt concentration was she aware of the attractive virile man beside her.

"I think you've got it, Jana," he said in deep tones. "I think you see what it is about New Mexico. As time passes you may begin to see more of what drew Lee to this place—you can see the color in the sky and the mountains. Now if you can just see it on the canvas, in the art, you'll have it made. Watching people come to New Mexico is very often like watching them fall in love."

Embarrassed, Jana withdrew into a shell of propriety. "Perhaps I'd better see the rest of the house now. It's been a long day and I should get some sleep."

Fletcher took her by the hand and pulled her to her feet. "Perhaps you should." They carried the plates and glasses back into the kitchen, where Jana made some efforts to wash up—efforts that were firmly repulsed by Fletcher.

"Leave it to Maria. She'd be offended if we did her

work for her. She has a lot invested in the idea that she takes care of us."

Us, Jana mused drowsily as Fletcher led her by the hand down the hall to what could only be the bedroom. What *us* is he thinking of?

Jana followed him through the low curved wooden door into a room which was stunning in its simplicity. The walls were white stucco, of course, and the floor was a terra-cotta Indian tile, its bare expanse softened by the colorful Navajo rugs that were beautiful enough to be hanging on the walls. When Jana skirted around one to get to her suitcases Fletcher reprimanded her gently.

"Lee always thought that beautiful things were to be used and enjoyed, not just admired. When you walk on this rug you will be fulfilling its original purpose. Try to think of it that way."

When Jana looked at him questioningly Fletcher responded, "Does it bother you to sleep in this room? There's the guest room down the hall, and then, of course . . ."

The implication roused Jana completely, and with a show of false pride she determined to hide her misgivings. "I'll be fine. The first night in a new place is always difficult, but I'm sure I'll get used to things quickly enough."

"I'm sure you will," Fletcher replied, his eyes darkening. "Well, I'll leave you to it." Before she could say a word he came forward and touched her lips with his. Too surprised to respond, she found herself vaguely disappointed when he quickly withdrew.

As she looked around the room a moment later she found herself thinking of their enchanting picnic dinner. Had she only imagined it, or had there been a real closeness there? She remembered the feeling of his strong, warm hand on hers as he led her down the hall to the bedroom. And after she had refused his desultory offer to share the bed in his studio she was surprised that he still kissed her good night. She shivered, remembering the pressure of his lips on hers, and with a thrill of excitement she knew it was a feeling she wanted to have again and again.

"Careful now," she said aloud as she headed toward her suitcases. "You're getting carried away. I guess they don't call New Mexico the Land of Enchantment for nothing."

Jana took out a warm nightgown and her fleecy velour robe and headed down the hall to the bathroom to brush her teeth and wash her face. The cold water invigorated her and she went back to the room to unpack, thinking that the activity would at least give her a head start on the day to come. She hung her clothes in the closets, noticing that they had been emptied in preparation for her arrival.

She crossed the room to the antique desk and began to put away her papers, checkbook and pen. Opening the desk drawer, she found an untidy clutch of papers. She knew that she should just put them aside in a neat stack, but she couldn't help noticing the name written in a strong handwriting that she already recognized from reading over the gallery's records. Almost as if she were under a spell she began to read what was only a fragment of a letter.

. . . As you know, I have worked very hard to get the gallery to the point where it is today

*and I would be guilty of false modesty were I to
say that I'm not pleased with my achievements.
Now that I'm getting older, though, I worry
about the future of it all. Santa Fe is not what it
used to be and so much of the art world here has
become superficial and competitive. I have such
faith in Fletcher in so many ways—we have been
each other's good luck, in a way. And for me, of
course, he's been the son I never had. But now I
just don't know. If he could only work through
this business with Taylor . . .*

And there the letter stopped. It was only a small
sheet of stationery, obviously taken from the middle of
a longer letter, and Jana could find neither the preceding nor the following pages. She sank back onto the
comfortable desk chair, puzzled. Had her aunt been
on the verge of losing her confidence in Fletcher
Logan? And if so, was it confidence in him as an artist
or as a man? Surely the latter, for his artistic talent was
evident enough. And "this business with Taylor"?
What business? Jana sighed, thinking that it could
only mean one thing. She remembered Taylor's
slim elegance, her poised confidence and, most of all,
her pride in her position within the Santa Fe community. Fletcher must be in love with Taylor.

Jana sighed with a combination of despair and
relief. At least now she had enough information to
keep from making a fool of herself. Any relationship
she had with Fletcher would have to be strictly
business in nature. She must have imagined that
closeness during the sunset. But she knew now that
she had lost something. Illusions—or was it hope?

She wearily turned to the low bed and drifted off to sleep.

The smell of morning coffee drifted down the hall and woke Jana from her sound sleep. She looked at the alarm clock and saw to her dismay that it was already eight o'clock. Springing out of bed, she hastily pulled her bathrobe around her and hurried down the hall to the kitchen.

In her heart she hoped against hope that Fletcher was making those comforting kitchen sounds, but somehow she doubted it. And anyway, what could she say to him, how would she act around him, knowing what she knew now? Well, she would have to face those piercing dark eyes sooner or later. It might as well be sooner. She steeled herself and walked through the door to the kitchen.

A comfortable maternal figure, dressed in jeans and a red sweater, turned to greet her. "Good morning," said the woman. She gave Jana a warm glance from her soft brown eyes and a welcoming smile.

"Good morning." Jana returned her smile.

"You must be—"

"I am—"

They both began simultaneously, then laughed together to cover the awkwardness of the moment.

Suddenly, Jana felt perfectly at ease; it seemed that it would be difficult indeed to feel uncomfortable around this woman. "I'm Jana Fleming. And you must be Maria."

"Of course. I've been expecting you for a long time. Sit down and let me give you some breakfast. You must be exhausted after the long trip, as well as the excitement of settling in here." Maria poured Jana a cup of coffee. "Cream or sugar?"

"No, thanks. Black is fine. It smells so good. I don't ever remember coffee smelling so good. It must be this cool desert air." Jana gratefully accepted the steaming cup and looked around again.

For the first time she was really able to appreciate the beauty of her surroundings. Through the french doors to the courtyard she could see extraordinarily green desert plants placed in gracious relation to the large elegant metal sculptures so that the overall effect was that of a tiny outdoor museum.

Jana smiled gratefully as Maria placed a steaming plate of scrambled eggs and bacon before her and fell to with a hearty appetite. Maria then poured herself a cup of coffee and sat down opposite. "Well," she said expectantly, "how do you like Santa Fe?"

Grateful for the opening, Jana found herself describing her first impressions of the town, as well as her first sight of the ranch. But all through her chatter her eyes kept straying to the door that led to Fletcher's quarters, a dozen unspoken questions lurking in her mind and, unbeknownst to her, in her eyes as well.

Following her glance, Maria broached the subject. "Fletcher already left this morning—very early, in fact. Miss Randall came by; she said a friend of hers, an important art critic from New York, had come in for the weekend and she thought it was important for him to meet Fletcher. He didn't seem too happy about it, but he went."

"I can imagine," Jana said drily.

"It's very hard here, you know, for artists. So many

come, but so few have real talent, and if you're good, as Fletcher is, you must seize every opportunity that you can." Maria had obviously overheard a number of conversations between Fletcher and Lee, Jana thought.

"Does Miss Randall come around much? I only met her yesterday; I don't know her very well at all." Jana was reluctant to pry, but she sensed that Maria would at least be honest in her reply.

"That one? She really doesn't spend that much time in Santa Fe. Or she didn't until she met Fletcher. She likes to think she discovered him, but in the long run she hasn't done him much good at all. Lee was really the one who brought Fletcher out, worked with him, made his career."

"Taylor's very beautiful," Jana ventured.

"That she is," agreed Maria and pursed her lips in a thin line. "If you care for the type."

Jana had had enough of this subject. "Well, I guess I'll dress and get ready for the day ahead."

Half an hour later Jana returned to the kitchen feeling renewed and refreshed. She had brushed out her hair, which was responding incredibly well to the desert air, curling exactly the way she wanted it to, and changed into maroon corduroy jeans and a nubbly pink sweater with a rough weave, worn over a crisp pink Oxford shirt.

"Aren't you a picture!" Maria obviously approved of her attire. "You'll blend right in with one of our fabulous sunsets!"

Jana blushed, thinking of her last sunset. "Why, thank you," she answered, hoping she at least sounded gracious. The two women then spent a more businesslike half hour together discussing Maria's various household duties and the hours she kept. Everything seemed in order and Jana only hoped that Maria would be as happy at the ranch with her in residence as she had obviously been with Lee.

Finally she realized how much time had passed. She knew that there was no sense in lingering at the ranch and she was eager to get to the gallery, but she didn't have the slightest idea what to do about transportation. Trying to be nonchalant, she asked Maria, "By the way, is there a car for me to use?"

"Oh, how thoughtless of me!" Maria exclaimed with obvious chagrin. "Of course! Fletcher told me to tell you that if you couldn't wait until he returned to go into town you should take Lee's old car. It hasn't been driven a lot in recent months, but we've tried to keep the battery charged up and it's always been reliable in the past. It's parked out back; let me get the keys for you." She left the room swiftly, determined to make up for having forgotten.

Keys in hand, Jana walked around to the back of the house, where she found the car—only to discover that it wasn't a *car* at all, but rather a huge, bright red van. How strange, she thought to herself; the red van didn't at all jibe with her image of her aunt. She had never driven anything this big in her entire life! "But then," she told herself determinedly, "this is the beginning of my new life. And if I don't learn to drive this thing I may be dependent on Fletcher for too many things. The least I can do is learn to get from place to place on my own."

She climbed into the van, relieved to notice that it was an automatic rather than a standard, and felt more at ease. She started up the engine and drove away from the ranch. However, once she got to the first intersection she realized that she didn't have the slightest idea where she was going—and there were no signs. She cursed herself silently for having been so enamored of the scenery that she hadn't even bothered to notice what turns Fletcher had been making. Too proud to turn back and ask Maria for help once again, she decided to forge ahead, wishing she'd paid more attention, but deciding that it couldn't be too hard to get back to Santa Fe.

To her dismay she found that all the roads looked pretty much alike, but she kept going. Half an hour later she had to admit that she was completely turned around—hopelessly lost. It was when the clumps of mesquite all began to look alike that she finally got worried. She decided to drive to the next intersection, where perhaps she would find someone to get directions from. She knew that might be only a vain hope, for she had begun to sense that she was really out in the country, not the big city where there were filling stations with friendly attendants on every other corner. "I won't think about that," she told herself, "until I have to."

But she had to think about it much sooner than she had planned. Driving down the road, admiring the desert foliage, she heard a loud bang and the van began to careen wildly from side to side. A blowout!

"Oh, no!" Jana groaned. "That's all I need." She kept her wits about her, though, and managed to slow down and stop at the side of the road. "Although," she said to herself, "there's so little traffic around here that it doesn't really matter!"

She clambered out and went around to survey the damage. The van looked slightly ridiculous, leaning to one side as it was, and the tire was damaged beyond repair. Well, if she was going to be an independent businesswoman she might as well start being self-sufficient about other things as well, she thought. She knew the theory of changing a tire perfectly well, but she had never tried to put it into practice, having gotten around Boston on the bus. But if there was ever a time to start, this was it.

She opened the double back doors of the van and found a set of tools and the spare tire, pulled them out and set to work trying to figure things out. She began trying to jack up the large vehicle, but it seemed hopeless. She was either doing it wrong or she just wasn't strong enough.

She was leaning against the side of the van, taking a rest from her fruitless exertions, when she noticed a cloud of dust approaching down the road. Her heart leapt with relief. People! At last she would be able to get some help and be on her way.

But her hope rapidly changed to embarrassment when she recognized Fletcher's truck. And he wasn't alone—two other people were with him! Jana wished with all her heart that she could sink into the very earth, for she was sure that she made out Taylor's face at a distance. This was simply not fair!

The truck pulled to a stop next to the van and Fletcher and Taylor climbed out, accompanied by an impeccably attired, elegant man. "Need some help?" Fletcher called to her in an ironic tone.

"Oh, you poor dear," Taylor cried, her voice dripping sweetness. "You should never travel alone—not when it can possibly be avoided." She added this last with a proprietary glance at Fletcher.

"I didn't have much choice," Jana said tightly, trying to keep her voice level. Really, this was simply too much to bear.

Fletcher grinned at her good-humoredly. "This shouldn't be too much trouble. I see that at least you've made a good start."

"I did try," Jana said earnestly. "I just couldn't seem to make it work." She added, in a tone of anger, "Besides, Maria told me that you had been keeping this van in running order. I never expected this to happen."

"Well, I did keep it running," Fletcher retorted, "but it seems to me that no amount of careful maintenance can prevent a blowout. I think that the responsibility for that belongs more with the driver. Why didn't you look where you were going?"

"But I did!" Jana protested.

"Now, now," interposed the stranger. "If you two are going to stand here and argue about this perhaps I'd better get busy and change this tire myself."

Jana and Fletcher both looked at him and laughed; the idea was too ridiculous. The man was attired in a tailored beige suit, not at all the sort of thing one would wear to change a tire on a dusty desert road.

Jana was determined to rise to the occasion. "I'm sorry. I seem to have lost all my good manners with this frustration. We haven't even met. I'm Jana Fleming." She extended a slender hand, realizing only too late that it was covered with dirt and grease. She tried to withdraw it, but the stranger had already grasped it firmly.

"And I'm John Peckham. I'm only visiting Santa Fe for a few days, but if all the women here are as beautiful as you are maybe I'll try to extend my stay."

"Why, thank you," Jana said, blushing.

Taylor cleared her throat and stepped forward. "I think I'll wait in the truck, if you all don't mind. Standing out in the middle of the road isn't exactly my idea of a good time." She stalked away.

Fletcher rapidly took control of the situation. "John, I have an idea. Do you think you could drive the truck?"

"Why, I don't know," John replied, but the look in his eye betrayed the fact that he was certainly eager to try. "I wouldn't mind having a go at it, if you'd trust me. Not that there's much traffic out here."

"Great!" Fletcher replied. "Why don't you and Taylor take the truck and go on back to her house? I'll fix Jana up and drive her into Santa Fe and drop by later for the pickup."

"No problem," John replied, "but bring Jana with you. I feel I'm being deprived of a pleasure I haven't even had a chance to enjoy yet."

"We'll see," Fletcher said nonchalantly, extending the keys.

It was obvious that Taylor wasn't pleased with the whole plan, for she and John seemed to argue briefly before the truck sped away down the road. Jana and Fletcher turned to face each other, like fighters squaring off for the next round.

"So," said Fletcher, "where did you think you were going?"

54

"What a ridiculous question!" Jana felt anger rise within her. "I was going to Santa Fe, of course."

"Not so ridiculous a question," Fletcher replied evenly, "when you consider that this van is pointed in the opposite direction."

"Well, I know I did get a little turned around," Jana admitted, "but I was going to stop and ask directions from the next person I saw."

"Which might very well have been Maria. Don't you realize that the ranch is just over the next hill?"

Jana blushed again and remained silent.

"That's all right," said Fletcher, sensing her discomfort. "It's just that we were all worried. Marie told me when we got back to the house that you had left quite some time ago. She tried to call the gallery to ask you something about dinner, and when Tony said you weren't there yet she got worried. By the time I got home she was really in quite a state, blaming herself for not making sure you knew the way, or for not making you at least wait until I returned."

"I'm sorry she was concerned," Jana said, "but I felt quite sure that I could make it on my own." She realized that her excuse sounded more than a little lame under the circumstances.

"That's all water under the bridge now," Fletcher said with good grace. "Let's get this show on the road and see what we can salvage of the day." He turned his attention to the work at hand, which he accomplished with ease and speed. Within fifteen mintes the job was done and they were ready to hit the road.

As he slammed the back doors of the van shut Jana turned to him and said, "You don't really have to come into Santa Fe with me, you know. I could drop you off at Taylor's house and you could give me directions. I'm sure I could make it on my own this time."

Fletcher turned toward her with a flash of anger in his gray eyes. Pulling her to him, he wrapped strong arms about her and bent his mouth to hers in a long kiss. She felt her body melt against his and felt no shame at her response to him. This was pure passion. This was no gentle lover's kiss; this was the action of a man marking his woman, making her his. And Jana, who had dreamed of just this all her life, found herself acquiescing with her whole heart. The long savage kiss then deepened into one of exploration and searching while Fletcher held her next to him in a powerful embrace. Jana had never realized that a kiss could embody every nuance of sensuality and she gave herself up to the sensual exploration of his warm mouth on hers, his tongue parting her soft lips. His hands slid down to her hips, molding her slight frame to his with need and passion, and when he finally let her go she was shaking with desire.

But need was quickly followed by anger; this had to stop. She and Fletcher were—and would remain— business associates and nothing more.

4

Jana stood at the front window of the gallery, gazing out over the plaza where the first snowflakes were beginning to fall. The brisk winter weather and the snow-covered streets brought back memories of Boston, memories which still had a strong hold on her imagination. From time to time she was immersed in feelings of nostalgia for her life back East, for the orderly and serene existence which she had created for herself there. The New England fall and winter had always been her favorite times, times when she had felt renewed and invigorated and ready for the approaching busy season. It hadn't been a life without problems, of course, but those problems seemed tame compared to the ones she was facing now.

Slowly but surely Jana felt that she was learning her way around the business, though she was well aware of the one major problem that was always nagging at the back of her mind. The gallery was losing money. In spite of the fact that it had been a thriving business during the days when her aunt was still alive it had entered a sharp decline during the months it took the lawyers to find Jana and bring her to Santa Fe. A number of gallery artists had worked together to keep it open, but despite their best efforts, and subsequently her own, Jana was faced with impending financial disaster. She hoped that a few openings, major events for any art gallery, would provide the necessary capital to keep the business going. At least Tony didn't seem completely discouraged. When he and Jana had their weekly sessions over the books he would point out to her that the slow time was starting, that if she could just hang on until the next active season the gallery would no doubt turn itself around. Jana was grateful for his optimism and swore him to secrecy concerning the gallery's real financial state. This was one burden she truly felt that she had to bear alone. Even Fletcher must not know.

And Fletcher! That was another major problem for her. They constantly grated on each other's nerves, especially at the ranch, which seemed so much smaller than on that first day. The passion that had marked their early encounters was always there between them, but once Jana had become aware of the true financial state of the gallery she had decided that work should be her major concern. And since Fletcher was professionally involved with the gallery she didn't feel that she could mix business with pleasure, at least where he was concerned. Too proud and too unsure of their relationship to confide in him, she retreated into a routine of constant work, rebuffing his attempts to draw her out or spend time with her. Puzzled and angry by her repeated rejections, he eventually retreated. She was powerfully attracted to him—she knew it and she knew he knew it—but she needed a cool head for the time being. With so many unspoken things between them it was no wonder that their relationship was so difficult.

At times the very landscape even seemed alien and threatening. The rugged desert, the seemingly limitless horizon—these things sometimes left her feeling very small and exposed. Even the beautiful sunsets she had enjoyed now seemed to mock her. She was desperately afraid of failing and couldn't bear to think of the gallery going under.

Occasionally Tony Phillips provided a diversion for Jana, as if he sensed her concern over the state of the gallery. She found him to be a pleasant enough companion; he seemed to know everyone who was anyone in Santa Fe. He introduced Jana to other art dealers and often took her to openings. Frequently she saw Fletcher and Taylor together at these functions, very obviously a couple, very much the center of attention. Jana observed these functions closely, aware that Grayson Gallery had not had a major opening for some time. She knew that Fletcher would have enough new work for a show in the near future and she wanted to be sure that she could put together a celebration which would make him proud of her, an opening that would be a kind of homage to the legacy of her aunt. She knew too that by pouring all of her energy into an opening for the man's art she was sublimating her desire for the man himself.

Rousing herself from her reverie and determined to

get her mind off Fletcher, she turned from the window to survey the gallery. Everything was in place, neatly polished and dusted. It was still, to Jana's eye, the most inviting shop she had ever seen. Just the day before she had bought a wreath made of dried red peppers and it was hanging in the window. The red earth tones against the white of the snow outside matched, for her, the serenity and warmth of the gallery as opposed to the bitter cold outside. She felt warm and secure among these beautiful pieces of art. Time hadn't dulled the affection she felt for the place itself, nor for the objects within it. Now if she could just make some new purchases for the gallery . . . But first she would have to sell something of importance.

Seized by a sudden resolve to do something, anything besides going back to her desk to do that depressing paperwork, Jana strode purposefully back to the storeroom, hoping perhaps that she had overlooked something that might be immediately salable. Even though she and Tony had made a cursory survey of the stockroom's contents they might have missed something, and with the snow beginning to come down even harder she doubted whether a lot of customers would be rushing in today.

The stockroom was fairly clean and Jana sifted through its contents with dispatch. There were several lovely Navajo rugs, which she set aside for cleaning before putting them on display. The rest of the stock was nothing special, mostly pottery and silver jewelry that would undoubtedly have to be marked down before it would sell, but right now Jana felt that things marked "reduced" weren't exactly conducive to the successful image that she wanted to project.

Finally, over in the corner, covered with a cloth, she found what she must have been looking for without even knowing it—a painting of Fletcher's. How it had ever been overlooked she could not begin to imagine, as Fletcher's works were among the best-selling items in the gallery. She realized that this must belong to an earlier period of his career, for it contained none of the joy and color that she associated with the paintings of his that she was familiar with. It was a very angry painting—executed in shades of black, gray and blue. The inventory slip on the back identified it as "Mountain Storm," dated several years previously. Jana saw no reason why the painting should languish in the stockroom, especially since Fletcher's work commanded such high prices, and this, while not exactly uplifting or cheerful, was certainly an eye-catching, dramatic piece.

Taking the painting out into the light of the gallery, Jana saw that it was in excellent condition; only the frame would have to be dusted lightly in order to make it completely presentable. Armed with dustcloth and cleaner, she proceeded to do just that and then she set up an easel in the front window so that passersby would immediately see it. That would be a useful gauge for her. If people weren't attracted to it and curious about it while it was in such a prime position perhaps it would never sell. She would just have to wait and see.

Satisfied that she had done all she could for the moment, Jana settled herself in the office with the depressing pile of paperwork that she and Tony would be dealing with tomorrow, one of his days in the gallery. She was on her second cup of coffee—and her second stack of bills—when the bell on the front door of the gallery rang, letting her know that someone had just walked through the door. Jana's heart rose and she felt her spirits rise. Hoping that it might be Fletcher, despite her firm resolve to keep their relationship on a professional level, she pushed aside the bills and hurried to see. Fletcher occasionally brought her lunch at the gallery, saving her the necessity of closing it while she ran out for a bite to eat. This morning he had said that he would drop by with sandwiches. But surely it was too early for that.

Jana walked into the main room with a ready smile on her face. "May I help you?" she inquired of the man who was chewing on an unlit pipe and gazing with rapt intensity at the painting she had just placed near the window. So that *was* a good move, she thought, smiling inwardly.

"I'd like to look around for a bit, if I may," the man replied, introducing himself as Max Prentice. "I always come to Santa Fe on vacation and this is one of the places where I like to browse. Unfortunately my trip is almost over, but I thought I could steal a little time to do the one thing I always enjoy here."

"Of course, take your time," Jana replied, smiling graciously. She rather doubted that the man would buy anything. He wore gray lizard boots, a western shirt and a turquoise belt buckle—all so new-looking that Jana suspected he had just bought them in a store down the street. He belonged, she thought, on a dude ranch instead of in Santa Fe. She realized with surprise that she was capable not only of feeling like a native Santa Fean but thinking like one as well. In any case, this Mr. Prentice hardly appeared to be the type to know much about art.

Jana busied herself at the back of the gallery, surreptitiously observing the man as he wandered around, every now and then asking a question which surprised Jana by its naiveté. By now she knew the gallery's stock and its history very well and she answered every question with patience and in clear detail, even though she really thought that he was just browsing and wouldn't buy anything.

After about an hour Mr. Prentice came up to Jana and said, "That painting in the window—'Mountain Storm.' How much is it?"

Surprised by his interest, Jana made a show of consulting her inventory list, which didn't even mention the painting, and then bravely named a price that was a thousand dollars higher than anything else of Fletcher's. Surely the man couldn't be serious!

If she had been surprised by his interest, she was shocked by his response. "I'll take it," he said cheerfully. "But can you ship it to my home in New York?"

"Certainly," Jana replied, having become accustomed to this request, since Santa Fe was a major tourist center. She waited curiously to see how the man would pay for the painting. To her surprise he wrote a check for the full amount, drawn on a Santa Fe bank. At his insistence she called the bank and verified the check.

While she was writing down Mr. Prentice's New York address they began to talk comfortably, business having been taken care of. To her astonishment he inquired after her aunt, saying that he had met her on previous trips to Santa Fe, and Jana explained what had happened.

Prentice was sympathetic as he replied, "Well, I certainly wish you the best of luck. I want this gallery to stay in business. Even though I only make it to Santa Fe once a year or so I've always enjoyed coming in here and your aunt was always very kind to me. I'll make a point of stopping in on my next trip to see how you're doing."

"Why, thank you," Jana said, genuinely touched by the man's thoughtfulness and genuine concern. "I hope you will," she added. As she watched him shut the door behind himself and walk out into the freezing snow she thought, I hope we'll still be here.

Putting the receipts and the check away in the safe, Jana mused to herself that one never could figure the workings of human nature. Who would have thought that such a strange little man would turn out to be an old friend of the gallery, let alone a good customer? She remembered what she had thought when he first entered the gallery and was ashamed of herself for having judged him so hastily.

She did have to admit that he hadn't presented the image of a typical gallery frequenter. She had thought he looked more like a tourist than most of the tourists in Santa Fe and it turned out that he owned his own home here—not just a home, but one on Canyon Road, one of the most desirable streets in the community. And the bank had certainly seemed to recognize his name when she called to have the check verified.

Well, Jana thought, it just shows that it pays to be nice to everyone.

She returned to her paperwork with a new enthusiasm, confident that this sale was a good omen, perhaps the start of an upswing for the gallery. She was pleased with the professional way she had handled the situation. So absorbed did she become, now that she had more money to apply to the rapidly mounting pile of bills, that she didn't hear the bell on the front door ring as Fletcher entered the gallery and appeared without warning at the office door.

Jana looked up from her work, startled to find him so close. As usual, her heart raced at the nearness of his presence and she felt a treacherous response to his steady gaze. She pushed back her chair and resolved to bridle her passionate and unpredictable emotions.

He greeted her with an affectionate smile. "My, don't we look like the typical entrepreneur this morning! Still have any interest in food, or are you too busy?"

He truly was the most charming man she had ever known, she thought. "I'm never too busy for food, as you should know. Have you seen the grocery bill for the ranch lately?" Jana was bristling with excitement over the recent sale, but decided to save the surprise for later. Her face was flushed with color and success had made her all the more attractive.

"I should say I have!" he retorted, pulling her out of the chair behind the desk, looking her over from head to toe. The touch of his strong hands was gentle and Jana could feel his warm breath on her face. "If I thought you were putting on too much weight I'd let you know. I'd like to think you're just adjusting to our fresh air with an increased appetite."

"I am!" Jana laughed in return. "Now, what new delicacies have you brought for me to devour?"

"Black bean soup and *tortillas*. Fresh from Josie's," he replied. "Good hot Mexican food and some of your favorite apple pie."

"Oh, good." She pretended to swoon. "It's a wonder I'm not as fat as a cow!"

"Believe me, if you were, I'd let you know." Fletcher inspected her trim form with mock severity, his eyes twinkling with delight. "But I happen to think you're just fine the way you are."

"Only just fine?" Jana questioned. "I had hoped for a little more approval than that."

"Be careful what you wish for—you just might get it," he threatened as he began setting out the delicious lunch.

This last was said with such seriousness that Jana felt tingles all the way down her spine. She wondered if Fletcher had any idea what she really did wish for. She watched him as they sat side by side, sharing their lunch on the narrow desk, knees touching underneath. She couldn't spend a moment in this man's presence without being aware of his physical attractiveness and she found it increasingly difficult to keep her capricious emotions in check. He seemed to radiate power and strength and she wished she could be closer to him. Several times she had thought of his close proximity at the ranch, realizing that so little space separated his quarters from her part of the house.

Lunch was consumed quickly as Jana and Fletcher discussed the details of their weekend plans. Jana had been working so hard in the gallery that she had had little chance to see much of New Mexico beyond Santa Fe and its immediate environs. Fletcher had promised to give her a tour of the surrounding area and had suggested that they go to Taos for the weekend and stop off on their way back to have dinner at Rancho Chimayo, a famous restaurant in a tiny village. Jana wasn't anxious to make the trip, for it would be the first time she had been alone with Fletcher for any length of time. She wouldn't be going at all if Tony hadn't been in the gallery when Fletcher suggested it. Tony had immediately offered to keep the gallery open for her, saying that Jana had been working much too hard. Jana had had no choice but to consent. She refused to leap ahead to the problem of staying in a hotel with him in Taos, trusting that he would somehow resolve that problem when they came to it. Nevertheless, she was filled with excitement and pleasure at the thought of having so much of his time and attention.

The arrangements had been made and Fletcher was now regaling her with tempting and vivid descriptions of the exotic plains covered with piñons and saltbush. He vowed she would never be the same after seeing firsthand the rugged rock formations of the Bandelier National Monument or the desert under a full moon.

"And do you promise a full moon?" she teased him.

"Of course. You don't think I make plans that I can't fulfill, do you? Besides, I consulted a calendar."

She laughed and wondered what had ever made her think she could say no to such an invitation. Indeed, what had ever made her think she could say no to Fletcher? Still, she had to keep trying!

After they had finished discussing their plans Fletcher rose as if ready to leave. "I'll just run this stuff back to the kitchen and dispose of it; you certainly don't want your office to smell like chiles all afternoon," he joked.

Jana stood also and went over to stand next to him. She thought he seemed reluctant to leave, that he was looking for reasons to stay on a bit longer. Surely it was her imagination, she chided herself. No doubt he had more important things to do than visit with her. Wondering if now was the right time to tell him about the sale of "Mountain Storm," Jana trailed after him into the tiny kitchen.

There were no windows in the small room. Jana felt as if the two of them were cut off from the rest of the world. She could hear the wind howling outside and knew the storm was gathering strength. The snow would be getting deeper by the minute and the chances for customers on such an afternoon were slim. She was momentarily uncomfortable as she realized how alone they were.

"Here, let me help you," she said, taking the dirty dishes from him and turning toward the kitchen sink.

"Now don't tell me that's woman's work—not a professional art dealer like yourself." Fletcher's voice was teasing as he relinquished the stack of dishes to Jana.

"Of course not," she retorted, obviously pleased with the compliment. "But you brought the food. Next time I cook, you wash."

Fletcher leaned against the counter as Jana filled the sink with soapy water. "Now this is the life. A good meal, a beautiful woman doing the dishes. What man could ask for more?" He smiled at her with apparent pleasure and she felt herself blush under the heat of his gaze.

"Not so fast," she teased back. "You're not getting off completely. Let's see if you're as good with a dish towel as you are with a paintbrush." She tossed a dry towel at him and he caught it just before it hit the floor.

"I thought there had to be a catch," he said as he dried the plate Jana handed him.

His hand touched hers as he took the plate and a flash of electricity sparked between them. The tenderness of his unexpected touch seemed to surprise him as much as it did her, and they finished the few dishes in silence, neither one wanting to break the spell between them. Jana's heart raced with sheer delight at being so close to Fletcher, whose masculine arm brushed against her own as they worked side by side.

She let the water drain from the sink as he put away the last dish. Wondering if she should tell him now about this morning's triumph, she felt his hand at her waist. She caught her breath as he turned her around to face him, his sensual lips coming down on hers, gentle and tentative at first until she returned his passion and they embraced with complete abandon. Jana felt his hand under her sweater and moaned deep in her throat as he clasped her closer to him. She leaned against the counter, arching her back, pressing her trembling breasts against his muscular chest and winding her arms around his neck. She gave in to desire as he teased her nipples into throbbing arousal and let the pulsating feeling overwhelm her. When he finally finished kissing her she rested her head on his shoulder and felt a shudder of pleasure go through her entire body as he kissed the back of her neck.

He released her gently and looked deep into her eyes. "Maybe we should go check on the storm. As much as I enjoy the thought of being stranded with you, I don't much relish the idea of being stranded here at the gallery. You eat entirely too much."

"Look who's talking." Jana laughed as she brushed her hair from her face, hot with emotion and desire. Food was the farthest thing from her thoughts at the moment. Why couldn't she keep her treacherous desires in check? She knew that she wanted to keep their relationship on a businesslike level, but her body kept betraying her.

Fletcher had turned off the light in the kitchen and turned to walk out into the gallery, holding her hand with his. Suddenly he looked into the open stockroom, an expression like thunder on his handsome features.

"And where did this come from?" he demanded in a voice filled with fury. He strode over to "Mountain Storm," which Jana had placed just inside the door in preparation for packing and shipping to New York.

Jana, struck by the hard anger in his voice, wasn't quite sure how to respond. "Well," she began hesitantly, "I had hoped to surprise you."

"Well, you certainly did," he thundered back at her. "Now answer me. Where did this piece of trash reappear from? What depths did you drag it out of?"

Jana was furious. What right did he have to display such anger? Determined to stand up for herself, she mustered all the courage at her disposal and said, "For your information, that particular painting, whatever your personal feelings about it, just brought in more money than anything we've sold this month. Perhaps the profit will comfort you."

"What?" Fletcher asked. "Do you mean someone

actually bought this piece? Why it's practically worth-less—the worst thing I've ever done! You of all people should certainly have sense enough to see that!"

"Fletcher," Jana retorted icily, "no matter how highly developed my artistic taste might be, a sale is a sale is a sale. And Max Prentice seemed to think it was worth the price."

Fletcher's jaw dropped in amazement. "Do you mean to tell me that you actually sold this piece to Max Prentice?" He started to laugh in a tone of true disgust.

Jana, stung, said with disdain, "Say what you will. I take anyone seriously who's ready to write a check on the spot."

"I just bet you do," Fletcher returned, lip curled. "Never mind that Max Prentice could afford to write a check for this entire gallery and never even miss the money. He has one of the finest art collections in the country—he probably bought 'Mountain Storm' as a joke!"

But Jana refused to be ashamed of what she had done. "He actually seemed quite taken with it, Fletch-er. So I'm afraid you'll just have to give up this artistic pretense of possessiveness. Better that it be in a famous collection than in a gallery stockroom."

"You!" Fletcher spat with disdain. "What do you know about art?" He turned on his heel and walked away, but not without turning to get in one last dig. "I suppose you'd sell me too, if you had the chance."

At this Jana's composure broke. All of the pride she'd felt in making a major sale suddenly deserted her and she was no longer able to hold back the tears. She heard the front door slam and ran to lock it behind him. She couldn't face another customer this afternoon.

Wanting to do what was best for the gallery, she went back to the office to call Tony. She struggled to keep her voice level as she asked, "Tony, do you think you could come over and mind the store for a while this afternoon? I really think I'd like to go home." Tony only worked part-time, but he had often offered to help out should Jana need a break.

"Sure, Jana." His calm voice was reassuring. "What's wrong?"

"It's nothing," she said with false cheer. "I'd just like to get a few errands done."

"Well, it's a smart thing for you to leave early if you want to make it back to the ranch. This snowstorm looks like it's going to be something. I'll be right over."

"If you don't mind I think that I'll just lock the front door and get started. Let yourself in with your key. And, Tony—thanks a lot."

Jana hung up the phone before he had a chance to ask any more questions, gathered up her things, locked the front door and left, hoping that no one would see her on the street. The tears were rushing down her face in earnest now and she knew that the only thing she needed was to be alone.

5

Jana drove along the snowy roads. She knew that she had done the right thing; she just knew it. And as far as she was concerned she was only acting with good business sense: a sale was a sale was a sale. If Fletcher hadn't wanted the painting sold why had he left it there at the gallery?

But deep in her heart she knew that there was much more to it than that. Their relationship constantly vacillated between the personal, with the almost uncontrollable passion that flared between them, and the professional—the area in which Jana felt most vulnerable.

"Perhaps," she said aloud mournfully, "I'll never fit in here." But even that was not the final truth. Jana thought of Fletcher as she had come to know him—his gentleness coupled with the volatile nature of an artist, the softness of his touch mingled with the strength of his arms, the warmth of his sensual lips and the coldness of his last angry words. Contradictions, yes, but beneath the handsome and polished facade seen by the rest of the world she saw a complicated, sensitive man with an inner vision all his own, an inner vision as distinctive as the signature on his paintings. He was not a man she could dismiss easily.

"I must be falling in love with him." The thought was so startling that she spoke it aloud again. And with that realization her heart rose. So this was what it was like. All these years she had never thought she would really be able to fall in love. She had known a number of men in Boston, but for the most part they were subdued, gentle, intellectual types who never made demands. Fletcher demanded a lot of her—things that she wasn't even sure she was willing to give. But because he demanded so much she was stretching, growing to become the person she had dreamed of someday being.

Jana pulled the van sharply to the left. She was straying too near the edge of the road. She remembered the letter written by her aunt and her heart sank. Thinking of Taylor Randall, remembering, for the most part, all of her doubts about herself, gave Jana a jolt. She realized that her self-confidence was still precarious. Could Fletcher ever care for her? Or was he only swept away by the physical attraction they could not ignore? If he cared for her at all, he wouldn't have been so easily angered. No, she had to dismiss any ideas about real affection and concern on his part. If she did indeed love him she must be resigned to a one-sided affair.

Jana shook herself from her reverie. You know better than this, she told herself as she took note of her surroundings. The snow was coming down hard and fast and the car windows were fogging over. If you really want him you have to fight for him. And if you want the gallery you have to fight for it, too.

Her determination was matched in strength by the blinding intensity of the storm raging across the desert, great waves of snow sweeping across the road. Jana wiped the fog from the window in front of her. She could feel the icy cold of the storm through her suede gloves. She had been so lost in her own thoughts that she had misjudged the intensity of the storm.

The world around her was a vast expanse of snowy whiteness and the sky looked as if it were filled with more bad weather to come. Jana, used to driving in the snow in Boston, wasn't too worried, especially when she realized that she was at most only a few miles away from the ranch. She knew her way around this countryside now. Its hills and curves and rocky shadows no longer looked the same to her. Each curve in the road was familiar, each plateau a signpost. As she had come to know Fletcher Logan over the past few months, so had she come to know the desert, to accept it on its own terms without trying to change it. Neither Fletcher nor the desert would conform to the norm. Jana smiled to herself as she imagined Fletcher in a three-piece suit sitting at a desk in Boston. The image was ludicrous.

Realizing that she was getting colder, Jana turned up the van's very efficient heater. She reassured herself with the thought that the large van seemed to be purring right along. Soon she felt warm as toast, lulled by the warmth into a sense of security.

Jana relaxed a bit, thinking how good it would be to get back to the ranch and have a hot cup of coffee. She doubted that Maria would be there; she would probably have gone home to avoid being trapped by the storm. The fight with Fletcher seemed miles away. She would have to calm down and collect her thoughts before Fletcher came home. If he came home at all. But surely he would, if only to be sure that she was all right. Perhaps, if she were just relaxed enough, she could clear up this matter about the painting. After all, no matter what happened they were still living almost in the same house.

Once again Jana forced herself to take note of her surroundings. She had been driving along quite easily despite the deepening snow and she realized that she would have to watch closely now if she were going to keep from missing the turnoff to the ranch. In a few minutes she saw it up ahead. She maneuvered the big van around the corner with easy confidence, only to find that she had headed straight for a snowdrift of gargantuan proportions. Powerless to stop in time, she applied the brakes gently, and skidded into the drift with a soft thud.

What now? She forced herself to be calm despite the rising fury of the storm outside. Up ahead, on top of the hill, she could vaguely make out the outline of the ranch. She thought she could see a few lights, though she knew that might be wishful thinking. Thankful that she had bought her heavy blue parka for its warmth as well as its fanciful style, she began looking around the van for anything that might be helpful in this emergency. A few minutes later she had a flashlight, a heavy Indian blanket and a pair of ski goggles, left over, no doubt, from someone's trip to Taos and the nearby ski range. She looked out the windows at the gathering snow, wrapped the blanket tightly around her, slipped the ski goggles on, took a deep breath and opened the door.

The blast of cold air almost unnerved her, but she knew that she mustn't hesitate. Staying in the van would only make her more frightened. At least this way she was doing something. She pulled herself together and stepped out into the soft snow, which at this point was up to her knees. She knew that she had to hurry, but she fought to keep herself calm; panicking could only lead to disaster. She was thankful that she had worn heavy boots, long wool pants and a sweater under her parka. With the blanket and the goggles she just might have a chance.

After taking a moment to get her bearings, she marched off firmly into the storm, resolved to progress in a straight line. Jana knew all the horror stories about people wandering around in circles in snowstorms and freezing to death, but she knew that she could avoid that by being conscious of it. Giving no thought to the danger of traveling over the rocky land, now completely disguised by snow, she proceeded firmly and cautiously up the hill.

She had almost made it! She was at the top of the hill, where the wind and blowing snow were especially vicious, but she summoned up her last ounce of courage and energy and propelled herself the last few steps toward the door of the ranch. After fumbling in her purse for the key, she tumbled through the door and, after a moment of relief and time to catch her breath, slammed the door, shutting out the blast of cold air and the flakes that were blowing into the house along with it.

What to do first? Jana threw off the wet blanket and hurried toward the back of the house. She hastily lit a fire in one of the fireplaces, got coffee started and headed for a hot shower and dry clothes. Instead of feeling shocked and exhausted she was rather proud of herself. She had done it.

The hot shower restored warmth to Jana's frozen body and she dried her hair quickly, fearing that she might catch a chill. She chose to wear a warm pair of heavy gray wool pants and a silk blouse, over which she donned a heavy, light blue cable-knit sweater. She felt like herself again as she brushed her silky hair and noted with satisfaction that the V-necked sweater fit flatteringly over her gently curving breasts.

The kitchen was warm and fragrant with the smell of fresh coffee. Jana downed two cups almost before she realized it and, having caught her second wind, looked about for something to rustle up for the evening meal. Deciding to attack the refrigerator, she found a note from Maria taped to the door.

Dear Jana and Fletcher,

I'm sure you'll understand that I've already gone home to my family. They say that this will be one of the worst storms we've had in years, so I wanted to be sure to make it home in time. Before I left I made a chicken-and-green-chile

casserole, which is in the fridge. I also made a
batch of fresh tortillas and a pot of beans, which
should be enough to get you through the storm.
I'll be in touch as soon as I can. Take care.

Maria

Jana was touched by Maria's thoughtfulness. There
was enough food for an army! Maria must have
thought that the storm would go on for days. Jana put
the casserole in the oven and placed the pot of beans
on the stove to simmer, then settled back in front of
the fire to drink coffee and watch the storm.

It was certainly getting worse. The snow looked like
a thick cloud surrounding the hill and Jana was
thankful that she wasn't trying to make her way up the
hill under present conditions. But then her heart sank.
Fletcher would face that terrible danger when he
arrived. In the euphoria she had felt over her safe
arrival she hadn't even thought to try to warn him.
Shocked by her thoughtlessness, she raced for the
phone and dialed the number of the gallery, hoping
against hope that he would somehow have gone back
there. The phone rang and rang, but there was no
answer. Cursing herself for not having thought of this
sooner, she dialed again, but the line crackled and
went dead. She couldn't get another dial tone. She
was completely alone, with no way to guess how long
the phone would be out.

In an effort to remain calm she forced herself to do
mundane tasks to keep her mind from dwelling on the
dreadful possibilities of the situation. She checked on
the casserole, then went back to the front of the house
and folded the blanket, wiping up the puddle of water

the melting snow had left on the floor. She peeked out the front door, but the snow was so blinding that she couldn't see a thing. Her heart sank. If Fletcher was out there she didn't have a chance of finding him herself. She had been lucky. What if he wasn't?

She turned on all the lights in the house, hoping against hope that if he were struggling up the hill this would help to guide his way. She lit fires in all the fireplaces, warming the house against the bitter chill, so that if he did arrive he would at least be warmed quickly.

Hours passed. Jana kept trying the phone, but it wouldn't work. She tormented herself with the terrible things that could have happened to Fletcher but knew that she was powerless to do anything. In a rational moment she told herself that Fletcher was certainly sensible, that he must have seen how bad the storm was and stayed in Santa Fe. In an effort to calm herself she poured herself a small brandy, thinking that she must keep her head. She placed the bottle next to the fireplace to warm, just in case he did come home, and curled up on the living-room sofa under a comforter, listening. All she heard were the sounds of the storm.

What was that noise? Jana shook her head from side to side. Despite the coffee, the brandy and the long trek up the hill must have taken their toll. She had dozed off on the sofa. But the noise! Perhaps the front door had blown open. Jana hurried down the hall, but the door was still firmly closed. She kept hearing the dreadful sound—it sounded like something was hurling itself against the heavy wooden door. Paralyzed with fright, the most dreadful thoughts ran through her mind. Perhaps it was some poor animal, trying to find shelter from the storm. She crept closer to the door and listened, trying to decide what to do. She thought she heard the sound of a human voice, a voice crying her name, though the sound was muffled by the storm.

She threw the door open and Fletcher tumbled through. It must be Fletcher, she thought, though the figure was so encrusted with snow that she could barely make out the human form beneath it. "Thank God!" he said in a husky voice, hoarse with the cold. "Thank God you're safe."

Jana rushed to his side and began peeling off his snow covered jacket and ski hat. His gloves were covered with snow and his fingers were so numb that he could hardly use them. Jana fumbled in her haste to help, for Fletcher was breathing rapidly and shallowly, obviously feeling the effects of his long journey through the snow.

When the two of them had finally managed to get off the wet and snowy outer layer of clothes Fletcher stood before her, shivering. "Are you all right?" Jana asked, hoping that the very real fear she had felt during those long hours of wishing that he were safely home didn't show.

"I am now," he said, looking at her with passion in his eyes. "If you only knew what I've been through, looking for you."

"I've been home for hours," she protested. "But that can wait. Let's get you some coffee and brandy." Jana felt him close behind her as they walked into the kitchen and she shivered. For the first time that night

81

she wasn't trembling from the cold. Never had she felt so close to him. Never had she felt so alone with him. The excitement of having him near made her whole body ache with pleasure.

He accepted the cup of steaming coffee heavily laced with brandy, downing it in one gulp. "I'll need some more of that," he said, "but first I'd better get out of these wet things and into a hot shower." And he went through the door that led to his part of the house without another word.

Jana busied herself in the kitchen, checking the food and making a fresh pot of coffee. She was tempted to go check on Fletcher, but since she had never been in his part of the house before she was loath to invade it now, especially since his condition was her fault—he could only be angry with her after searching for her so long.

After what seemed like an eternity she became worried, not having heard a sound from his part of the house. What should she do? Thinking that she had nothing left to lose, she poured a fresh cup of coffee and brandy to take to him.

The room she entered was magnificent in its austerity. The white walls were covered with paintings and there was another one shrouded on the easel. But Jana was determined not to stop—she had to make sure that Fletcher was all right. She went down a narrow hall and passed the bedroom, where she noticed a huge bed, as well as a small fire glowing in the *posada.* Surely he couldn't still be in the shower? She went on to the bathroom; just as she raised her hand to knock, afraid of the silence within, the door opened and Fletcher stood before her, clad only in a towel knotted about his waist.

Jana was stunned and embarrassed by the position she found herself in and even more embarrassed by the fact that she couldn't seem to stop looking at him. "I brought you this," she murmured, holding out the coffee. "I was worried when you took so long."

As casually as if this happened every day Fletcher took the cup from her hand, took a long gulp and placed it on the small counter behind him. Jana watched him in silence, her eyes taking in his every movement. His powerful chest was covered with curls of soft dark hair and Jana found herself longing to touch him. His powerful shoulders and torso tapered to a narrow waist and his muscular legs were all too evident beneath the brief wrap. Jana felt herself lose all willpower as he reached for her and she accepted the inevitable as it came.

His strong hands spanned her waist as he drew her to him. Lost in the compelling moment, Jana had no choice but to comply. His mouth came down on hers in a probing, searching kiss and Jana could taste the flavors of coffee and brandy as his tongue crept through her parted lips in exploration. Almost without her realizing it her arms went around his neck as the two of them were fused together in a passionate embrace.

Jana was conscious only of their mutual desire as his hands crept under her sweater and shirt to caress the soft skin beneath. Gently, gently, his hands roamed upward to caress her breasts, teasing them to arousal until she was moaning with her need for him. She could feel his strength through the thin towel and she began to tremble, all fear and rationality gone for the moment. She felt totally alive, aware only of the delicious things he was doing with his hands and mouth.

Fletcher didn't cease his fevered exploration of her body as he picked her up and carried her into the bedroom, placing her gently on the large bed in front of the fire. With her willing assistance he carefully removed her sweater and unbuttoned her blouse, stroking her breasts as he easily removed her bra. Her nipples hardened beneath his touch and Jana twisted and moaned beneath his insistent hands. Cupping both breasts between his hands, he put first one nipple in his mouth and then the other. As Jana arched her back to meet his mouth her hands found his chest and the hard male nipples. A shudder raced through his body at her intuitively perfect touch and he buried his face between her soft, full breasts. Completely aroused, Jana tried to reciprocate, but he firmly pushed her back down on the bed, tormenting her with his hands and mouth and tongue until he had taken off all her clothes. Finally, when she lay there totally undressed, aroused in every cell, he withdrew from her, standing up, his magnificent form framed by firelight. Untying the single knot which held the towel in place, he let it fall to the floor.

Jana was stunned by the sight of him. His pose was not arrogant, merely inviting. He was allowing her to look at him, to admire him, just as he was admiring her. Jana couldn't tear her eyes away, perusing with pleasure his perfect virile form. As he walked toward her their eyes locked in a gaze which was white-hot in intensity. It seemed to take forever until she felt his warm body settled on the bed next to hers.

He sought her with total abandon. Jana found that she was reticent at first, though glorying in Fletcher's relentless appreciation of every part of her. His searching lips and tongue traced first one breast, then the other, teasing her sensitive nipples into rosy peaks. "So lovely, so lovely," he murmured huskily and Jana could only gasp with pleasure as his questing hands sought the tender curve of her waist to find the sensitive flesh below.

He coaxed her to the edge of ecstasy with intermittently murmured endearments as he kissed and caressed every part of her. Jana had never known such passion, but she gave herself up to the heady experience as she began her own explorations. Her hands ruffled through Fletcher's hair, then over his strong shoulders, returning to his face, which she gently pulled up to hers. Looking up at him, she saw the desperate need in his eyes and knew that it was mirrored in her own.

At his urging she explored his body, the boldness of his need, her fingers delighting in the very texture of his skin, searching out the taut muscles beneath. The hair on his chest was damp and she licked one strong strong shoulder, detecting the salty taste of his skin. The two of them were beginning to know each other in the only way truly important to men and women— the time-honored code of passion, which they were obeying in all its dictates. Finally, when both of them were almost breathless with the pleasure of it, their bodies almost inextricably intertwined, Fletcher looked into her eyes and rasped, "Jana, I want you. . . . Now?"

Her eyes answered the spoken question with silent eloquence. He moved to join with her in a fevered explosion of need and desire. Her entire body arched upward to meet his thrusting conquest, moving in perfect rhythm as their bodies joined in the hot embrace. Language was totally unnecessary as they silently spurred each other on to greater heights of passion. At last, Jana could stand it no longer and her entire body seemed to explode in a paroxysm of pleasure and joy. She had never dreamed such delight was possible. Fletcher, his pleasure almost as much for her enjoyment as for his own, rocked her gently until his movements could be controlled no longer. The house was alive with the sounds of Jana's soft moans of pleasure and Fletcher's sharp cries of ecstasy.

Outside the storm raged about them in anger. Inside, much later, after both had slept for a while, Jana awoke to find Fletcher looking down at her, his delighted eyes searching her face. Sleepily she asked, "Aren't you hungry?"

"Of course," he answered, "but not for food." And his lips met hers tenderly and with a hunger that drove away all sensible thought. With reckless abandon she returned his kiss, her arms wrapped around his waist, her hands delighting in the muscular strength of his back. For a moment he moved away from her as if to study her face, which he held cupped in his hands. "I wonder if you realize how beautiful you are," he whispered before he took her in his arms once more, crushing her bare breasts against his chest. She gasped out loud as he kissed the back of her neck, his hands moving up and down her back. Sensing her need as well as his own, he gently eased her back onto the bed, kissing her lightly on her neck and throat, his fingers teasing her nipples into hardness before he bent down and caught them in his mouth, his tongue making circles on the sensitive skin.

This time their lovemaking was different. Unlike the fevered passion of exploration that marked their first coupling, this time they used their knowledge of each other's flesh to tease, to taunt, to experiment with ecstasy. Jana had never dreamed that such delight was possible as Fletcher caressed her, teasing her body into achieving ever-changing positions, each one more delightful than the last. Gone was any embarrassment on her part and she was both proud and amazed at the endless variety of her body's responses to this man.

Fletcher whispered appreciative, coaxing endearments as he tormented her already too-aroused flesh with new delights, watching her face for the dreamy, surprised looks he found there. Finally he eased her back onto the bed, plunging into her softness with barely leashed excitement. Overcome by the strength and power of his lovemaking, she let her hands roam over the length of his back, enjoying the play of muscles under her touch.

For a brief moment he drew his head back and looked deeply into her eyes; then his mouth came down to cover hers as he completed his sensual possession of her, the powerful movements of their bodies spurring them on to greater and greater levels of sensual knowledge and fulfillment. At last the tension snapped as they found their joint release, Jana's marked by a soft, whimpering cry answered by Fletcher's groan of fulfillment. The storm of passion over for the moment, they subsided against each other, exhausted, their damp bodies glistening in the firelight. They spoke in low tones, not wanting to break the spell of their mutual enchantment.

"I was so worried," she said.

"Well, I was worried too," he replied and reached out to tousle her already wild hair. "I went back to the gallery but you had already left. I guess your head start made all the difference. And all along the way there were these stupid tourists who hadn't the slightest idea how to drive in the snow. I ended up using the truck to push several of them out of drifts when I knew that all I really wanted to be doing was making sure you were all right. And when I saw the van at the bottom of the hill I got really scared, thinking that you were wandering around lost in the snow. So what did I do? Rather than being careful, I rushed out into the snow and proceeded to wander around in circles myself. It wasn't until I made a circle back to the van that I realized what I'd been doing. So I forced myself to be calm and take my bearings. After all, I know this country like the back of my hand. After I calmed down I made a beeline for the house, though by that time the going was really rough. And so here we are." He smiled down at her with warm affection.

"Yes." She smiled back. "Here we are. And to think that I was frightened that you wouldn't come home at all after that terrible fight at the gallery. Can you ever forgive me?"

"Of course," he returned readily. "But can *you* ever forgive *me?* Try to put it down to artistic temperament. I realize that you were only doing your best, but you have to remember that artists only want the world to see what they consider their very best work. That painting is all right, but it belongs to what I now consider a much more immature period in my work. I suppose, though, if things keep on the way they are now, that it will eventually have some value for collectors. So you did the right thing. It was just my stubborn pride standing in the way."

"Well, thank you for saying that." Jana smiled at him. "So from now on you be the artist and I'll be the dealer. Agreed?"

"Agreed. But is that all you really want to be?" With that his rough cheek grazed her face once again as he bent to kiss her.

"Whatever do you mean?"

"Well, ever since I met you I've been thinking that—" At that moment the phone in the kitchen rang shrilly.

"Damn!" he growled and, getting out of bed, raced for the studio.

Jana lay there wondering what on earth he had been about to say. She wondered who was on the phone, thinking that it must be Maria calling to check that everything was all right. But Fletcher's deep tones, carrying clearly through to the bedroom soon led to a different conclusion.

"Yes, Taylor," he said, "we're both fine. As a matter

of fact, Jana got home long before I did. . . ." His voice trailed off and Jana missed the rest of what he said.

As soon as Jana knew who was on the phone it was as if someone had dashed cold water over her. Trembling with anger, her joy at the previous hours forgotten in her jealousy, she quickly rose and dressed. Then she entered the kitchen, feigning nonchalance as she passed Fletcher, and started to get dinner ready. While she was doing so she couldn't help noticing the time; it was well after midnight. What a fine time for Taylor to call!

"Yes, of course, I'll see you as soon as I can, but remember, we all may be snowed in for a few days. Take care of yourself. Good-bye."

Fletcher strode into the room, seemingly unconscious of the fact that he was standing there completely naked. Jana, trying not to become aroused once again, busied herself at the stove, but he came over to her and put his arms around her. "Now why have you gotten up? Are you really that hungry?"

"Yes, I find that I am—now," Jana said stiffly and pointedly.

"Well, all right, I suppose I'll get dressed and join you, then. But I don't understand what you're so upset about. I thought we were having a lovely time."

"That's exactly what it was," Jana said to herself as he strode off to dress. "A lovely time—and it certainly won't happen again. Once was quite enough for me."

By the time she had gotten the food on the table Fletcher had returned, dressed in tight-fitting jeans and a sweater. Jana had to fight to keep her eyes from roaming over the now-familiar form, had to consciously suppress her desire to reach out and touch him. But, she kept reminding herself, he obviously belonged to Taylor. "Though it was hardly thoughtful of either of them to remind me of that fact when I was still in his bed," she muttered under her breath. She reproached herself for what she now saw as her wanton behavior, simultaneously excited and dismayed that despite her inexperience she had behaved with such complete passion and abandonment. She felt slightly shy with Fletcher, as if they were strangers now, instead of two people who had shared the act of love.

As the two of them ate the delicious food Maria had left for them Fletcher tried to make small talk several times, but every time Jana refused to respond. Finally the two of them subsided into a tense and strained silence.

After they had had dinner and coffee Jana rose to do the dishes and clean the kitchen, but Fletcher reached out to stop her. "Surely we can think of something better to do."

Ignoring the innuendo, Jana continued her work. "I certainly can. After I clean this up I'm going to bed—alone."

"Well, if that's the way you want it, Jana. It's a dangerous game you're playing—and I don't like it—but for tonight I'll let you have it your way. Just keep in mind that if I decide I really want you there's not a thing that will stand in my way. I certainly know that you won't."

Jana, unable to hold back the tears for the second

time that day, fled the room, preferring to face her shame alone. She flung herself across the bed in her room, sobbing as if her heart would break, thinking that her part of the house certainly seemed lonely now. What had she done? she wondered endlessly as she cried herself to sleep.

6

Jana awoke the next morning feeling more than a little depressed. It was unusual for her to sleep badly, and for a few moments she was disoriented and confused. She twisted and turned a bit before she realized that she had spent the entire night sleeping in her clothes. No wonder she felt so uncomfortable!

A flood of memories rushed over her and she felt a sharp pang as her cheeks grew hot with memories of the previous evening—the relief at finding Fletcher safe after hours of worry, the closeness of their intimate hours together in front of the fireplace, the splendid moment of their need fulfilled. Her depression and embarrassment, however, had little to do with the act itself, for she remembered her lovemaking with Fletcher with an intense pleasure that made every inch of her body ache with longing. It was the aftermath that dismayed her and brought tears to her eyes.

How could she have been so foolish? How could she have believed for even one evening that Fletcher felt anything for her except physical attraction? How could she have thought that she could entice him away from the beautiful Taylor? And yet it was hard for her to believe she had merely been a convenience to him. He had been so gentle, so loving in his strength. Had she just imagined his ardent need of her? It all seemed so genuine—and yet there could be no doubt about his instant response to Taylor's call.

No. A thousand times no. She would just have to face facts, as difficult as it was. She had been there when he needed someone—anyone would have done. She mustn't be so naive as to believe it had meant the same to him as it had to her.

A quick glance in the mirror made it all too obvious that she had cried herself to sleep. She was aghast at her own transparency. She jumped into the shower and hoped that the warm water would at least wash away all the outward evidence of her emotional response to what had happened. She knew better than to hope for a total cure. That would take a long time.

Jana decided to wear a new wool sweater with her good wool slacks. She needed all the self-assurance she could muster this morning. This was no time to neglect her appearance. The pale blue outfit soothed her jangled nerves and the feel of the soft angora against her skin relaxed the tired tenseness of her body. Her slenderness was accentuated by the outfit and the color was becoming. She brushed her hair briskly until it bounced with a life all its own, and in a few minutes she was as ready to face the day as she would ever be. She could think of no further excuse to remain in her bedroom. Sooner or later she would have to face Fletcher, so it might as well be sooner, she thought to herself.

The pungent aroma of fresh coffee greeted her as she made her way down the hall toward the kitchen, but her reluctance to face Fletcher prevented her from enjoying the familiar early-morning smell. She wondered if Maria were there, but immediately knew the folly of her wishful thinking. The snowstorm had undoubtedly blocked all the roads, leaving Maria no way back to the ranch. Jana knew with a terrible certainty that she and Fletcher were alone together and never before had the spacious house seemed so small.

Jana steeled herself to face those ravaging dark eyes, eyes which now knew every part of her body. Instead the very emptiness of the kitchen mocked her and it was with disbelief that she surveyed the quiet room. A pot of coffee was simmering on the back of the stove and cinnamon rolls were warming in the oven, but Fletcher was nowhere to be seen. Jana hurried to the window and was surprised to discover a radiant sun and a brilliant blue sky overhead. The storm had relinquished its fury during the night. Surely the danger had passed! The snowdrifts looked deep, however, and Jana had to turn her face away from the brilliant glare of the sun's reflection on the snow.

She poured herself a cup of coffee to clear her head.

There, taped to the refrigerator door, was a note which read simply: "Be ready at ten. Taos is much lovelier when it's covered with snow."

Jana was amazed. Did he really expect to go to Taos today? In this weather?

At first she felt a childish resentment at the curtness of his note. What arrogance! Maybe first impressions were accurate, after all, she said to herself, thinking back to her first emotion-filled meeting with Fletcher at the airport. After last night, if he thought that she was going off to some remote mountain village with him for the weekend he was out of his mind.

Jana set her coffee cup down on the kitchen table with angry determination and, with a hotpad, reached in the oven for the cinnamon rolls. If he thought he could so easily twist her around his little finger he had another think coming. She had better things to do than run around the country at his whim.

But cool reason prevailed. The coffee was delicious and Jana could see Fletcher in her mind's eye, up early and making coffee. Her heart softened in spite of herself. She was making entirely too much of the previous evening; she was sure of it. This was hardly the age of Victorian morality, and if she could enjoy this pleasant interlude with Fletcher she would. After all, what was one weekend? Monday morning she would go back to work and face the same old problems at the gallery. She would once again be back in her professional role and *then* she would decide what to do about Fletcher. But for now . . . well, it was just an affair, that was all. It happened all the time! After all, she mused over her coffee, she was no longer the young innocent she had been the day before. And if she refused to accompany him he would know that she had been more than a little shaken by the intensity of the experience. She intended to give no man that satisfaction.

Breakfast filled her with new confidence. She was no longer the helpless young thing he had knocked down at the airport and she hadn't given up the security of her well-ordered life in Boston to be daunted so easily by a weekend trip to the mountains. She was no virgin, after all, she mused ironically.

After putting her dishes in the dishwasher, she saw that it was nine-thirty. She raced to her room, thankful that she had dressed so carefully this morning and that just the week before she had treated herself to a new pair of leather boots. She and Fletcher might never again be lovers, but at least she would have the confidence that every woman has when she knows that she looks her best.

It was a little after ten when she finished packing. Fletcher was nowhere in sight. Her van was parked outside, but Fletcher's truck was gone.

Of course! Where else? If Taylor had been able to distract him so easily the night before he had no doubt gone to see her that morning. Jana was filled with angry gloom, but she was more determined than ever to go through with this weekend. Perhaps Fletcher had gone over to make his excuses for not being able to see Taylor this weekend; he must be taking Jana to Taos out of a sense of obligation. She cringed at the thought of the two of them talking about her, but she took a savage pride in the fact that at least she would have Fletcher all to herself, whatever his motives were.

"What is it that man does to me?" Jana asked aloud

of the empty house. Never before in her life had she been filled with such jealous fury. Never before had she been so torn with endless turmoil. Sternly she lectured herself that she was above all this. Nothing could be so important, she fumed as she paced the kitchen floor. Nothing. Absolutely nothing.

"Who am I trying to kid?" she said, again out loud to the empty house. She knew she had been forever changed by the passion she had shared with Fletcher and her heart beat faster at the thought of his embrace, tender and strong, virile, bold.

Just then she heard the familiar roar of his truck and she quickly sat down. Her heart raced in spite of her efforts to appear calm as he strode into the kitchen, whistling happily. All her attention was directed to her cup of coffee, as if she had been lingering there all morning.

"Good morning," he said warmly, looking her over and quite obviously approving of what he saw.

Jana was furious at the blush she felt rising in her cheeks. "Good morning yourself. How's the snow situation?"

Fletcher was nonchalant. "Actually, it's not nearly as bad as we thought. The radio said it was one of the worst storms ever. But the roads seem clear and I'm sure we'll have no trouble making it to Taos."

In spite of her determination to appear sophisticated Jana's forthright honesty got the best of her and she blurted out, "Fletcher, are you really sure that you want to go through with this?"

Looking at her with puzzlement, Fletcher answered, "Of course. I did promise. Besides, I can't imagine anyone I'd rather spend the weekend with."

He moved toward her, but Jana never had a chance to find out what his true intentions were, for she rose and busied herself with the coffeepot, then turned off the stove and the lights in readiness for the trip. Fletcher shrugged and proceeded to carry her luggage out to the van. Jana, having sensed that she had delayed as long as she could in the house, locked up behind them and joined him.

"I thought that this would be the most comfortable way for us to travel today," Fletcher explained. "The truck might have been a little faster in the snow, but I think that this is more comfortable. Besides, I'm in no hurry. Are you?"

Jana knew he was gently teasing her, chiding her for being so restrained, so distant. She tried vainly to respond in a lighthearted fashion to his comfortable banter. She was glad to be riding beside him in the van, thrilled by his masculine touch when he helped her up onto her seat, wrapping a wool throw across her lap. But she was confused by the range of new and unfamiliar feelings she had experienced in the last twenty-four hours. It would take time for her to relax enough to respond any differently.

Jana was delighted that Fletcher was driving. The road down the hill, though clearer than she had expected, was slippery and the snowbanks on either side were huge. Even so, she was uncomfortable at being trapped in such close quarters with Fletcher. Tension crackled between them as they stared straight ahead, neither looking at the other. He wanted a definite response from her and she found that she was unable to give it.

Abruptly, they both began to speak at once.

"Isn't it—?"

"Do you think—?"

Jana plunged ahead with what she thought must surely be an idiotic question. "Do you really think that the roads will be clear all the way?"

"I hope so," Fletcher replied. "After all, a substantial part of Taos's livelihood comes from the ski trade. In beautiful weather like this it's certainly worth it to keep the highway open. And after all, the storm *wasn't* as bad as we thought."

"It seemed pretty bad to me," Jana said, but she didn't want to dwell on the awful fear she had felt while out in the storm and then, later, her terrible fear for Fletcher. She didn't want to talk about the night before at all.

As if he were reading her mind Fletcher spoke gently, reaching across the seat to take her hand, "Jana, about last night . . ."

Withdrawing her hand from his warm clasp, Jana stiffened and looked out the window. "Fletcher, I really don't want to talk about it. Not now. Not ever."

"Honey, sooner or later we're going to have to talk about it. It wasn't just one of those things, you know."

"That may be true, Fletcher," Jana spoke softly, unable to meet his eyes, "but somehow I don't think that this is the time or the place. And I don't think that I'll want to talk about it for quite a while. All right?"

"Very well," Fletcher said, his lips tightening. Never had his self-control been more evident. "But we may have to talk about it sooner than you think, Jana. It was too important."

Jana didn't respond. With a real effort of will she kept from trembling, pretending interest in the scene outside. Her thoughts raced a mile a minute. What was there to talk *about* really? That she had responded to him as only a woman in love could respond to a man? How would they ever be able to work together again? These were things Jana knew she must face eventually, but she didn't see any reason why she had to discuss them with Fletcher—it was hard enough to face them by herself. She couldn't soothe his guilty conscience as well.

Stealing a glance at him, she couldn't help wondering why he thought last night had been so important. Then she decided that he had probably realized that she was relatively inexperienced, and felt responsible. She was more determined than ever to pass it off as if it were nothing important. That was her only hope of salvaging what remained of her flagging self-respect.

Rousing herself from her reverie, she began to talk about the landscape outside. If Fletcher was surprised at her matter-of-fact tone he disguised it and was soon discussing the scenery and Taos with her as if they were the best of companions.

"It is lovely, isn't it? Once you get up to the mountains of Taos you realize what being high really means. Be careful not to get too dizzy, especially in this cold air. And don't expect too much of the place. After all, most people who are truly fond of Santa Fe are fiercely loyal to it and don't understand what all the fuss is about Taos."

"But I had always thought of Taos as a leading art center," Jana replied.

"So do most people. And Taos is really the place that started it all. Imagine what it must have been like back in the twenties, trying to get here before the freeway was around. It was truly remote then. You had to *want* to get to Taos or it wasn't worth the trip."

"A lot of people must have wanted to get there, though."

"You bet! And once Lawrence and O'Keeffe made their marks in literature and art, tourists flocked to the place. One of the lesser-known tourist attractions, even these days, is a room in a small hotel which contains the erotic paintings of D.H. himself. But, of course, the person who really got them all to Taos in the first place was that crazy Mabel Dodge, the wealthy eccentric who persuaded Lawrence that New Mexico was really the place where he could do his best work. I imagine she wasn't too happy when Frieda come along to keep an eye on him."

Jana fell silent, her thoughts returning to the man by her side. She was overcome by the thought that there were so many things she wanted to know about him and now, she thought, she might never know them. She had to keep this relationship on an even plane. She had already lost her heart to him—the only hope she had now was to keep from making a complete fool of herself.

Before she realized it they were pulling into the central plaza of Taos. Jana was enchanted by the sight of this tiny town nestled among the mountains, but she knew in her heart that she would always prefer Santa Fe.

"Everyone must be off skiing," Fletcher said when she commented on the emptiness of the area. "Perhaps we'll take a run out to the basin later and look around. Do you ski, Jana?"

"No," she replied, "though I'd like to learn. It's a shame to live so close to a resort like this and not take advantage of it, don't you think?"

Fletcher grinned. "Right. And I know just the person to teach you."

"And I guess I'm looking at him right now." Jana laughed into the warm gray eyes of the man beside her.

"Right again."

Jana felt a thrill of delight shiver through her body at the intensity of his incredible silver eyes gazing at her with such enthusiasm. It was going to be even harder than she thought to keep this relationship on an even keel. Her own emotions betrayed her again and again. She turned her eyes to the picturesque little town and remarked on its loveliness.

"You're seeing it at its best," Fletcher returned. "In the summer Taos is just another dusty little desert town."

Jana replied with true appreciation, "I'm glad to be seeing it at last."

"I should think it's high time you took a break," he flashed back. "You spend far too much time at the gallery and when you're not there you're always worrying about it. That's no kind of life for a woman like you."

The afternoon passed quickly. After a drive to the ski basin, a tour of a famous artist's studio and a trip to the Taos Bookshop, where Jana purchased several volumes on local history, among them a prized set of Mabel Dodge's memoirs, the day was drawing to a close and the sky was beginning to darken. Jana couldn't help feeling thrilled with all the things she had discovered during the afternoon. And Fletcher's hand on her shoulder as they studied a painting together, his arm around her as he guided her through a door, his face close to hers as they looked at books were comfortable and natural. More than once she longed to reach out and touch him, to lean her cheek against his, to hold him close. She hoped the day would never end. And wondering how—and *where*—the day would end was more than a little disconcerting.

Although it was late Fletcher insisted on taking her to see D. H. Lawrence's erotic paintings. On entering the somewhat dingy hotel lobby, Jana was shocked that such famous paintings were housed in such strange surroundings. After paying the dollar viewing fee, they were led into a tiny room which obviously functioned as an office. A lot of the walls were taken up with space for filing cabinets and the entire baseboard was lined with shoes.

As for the paintings themselves, Jana was surprised to find that she was not in the least moved by them. She saw them as objects of curiosity rather than true works of art. She had been afraid that they would be truly erotic and that it would be embarrassing to view them with Fletcher, but that was not a problem. She was more amused than anything else.

Sensing that Fletcher was waiting for her opinion, Jana decided to say what she truly thought. "Well, it's a good thing Lawrence was such a terrific writer," she commented.

Fletcher responded with uproarious laughter. "I knew you'd say that. You wouldn't believe how many people come here and rant and rave over what a terrific lost talent Lawrence was! I should have known you wouldn't be fooled. Still, they are interesting, especially if you've read his work."

"They certainly are," Jana replied, concealing her relief at his response to her comment. She should have had more faith in herself. Apparently all those months of working with artists had taught her a lot, more than she gave herself credit for.

They left the hotel, laughing together, and strolled out into the beautiful purple twilight settling around them. Jana felt herself grow tense wondering what accommodations Fletcher had made for that evening. They had planned this trip weeks ago. Maybe he had made two reservations. Her rational self told her that she hoped he had—but her heart remembered with pleasure his passionate exploration of her body the night before. She felt weak and scarcely trusted her own legs. She fully understood what it meant to be completely swept off her feet and had to force herself to return to reality.

"And now, my fine tourist guide," she said in a slightly mocking voice, "what have you planned for dinner?"

The look he gave her was mysterious. "That's my own surprise!"

Jana did her best to quell the feelings of alarm that rose within her. What harm could there possibly be in having dinner with Fletcher? Even a romantic candle-light dinner, if that was what he had up his sleeve. They did, after all, share a house. She couldn't start running scared at the slightest provocation.

"Sounds like fun," she said, attempting to sound casual, and settled back into her seat to enjoy the ride through the snow.

To her surprise Fletcher headed back toward the Santa Fe highway. Shortly after reaching the main road, he turned down a narrow country road and headed into the snowy whiteness. The road was unmarked, so she had no idea where they were, and she pretended not to notice they were traveling farther and farther from the town's center. A few moments later Fletcher turned down a narrow lane that led to a magnificent adobe compound composed of several beautiful buildings, all encircled by a low adobe wall.

"What is this place?" She was overwhelmed by its magnificent isolation; against the snow it looked like some incredible fortress. Surely this must be one of the resplendent desert retreats of the wealthy that she had read so much about.

Fletcher parked the van in front without answering her question. With deliberate silence, as if not wanting to break a magical spell, he came around to help her out into the slippery snow. Together they walked across to the door in the low adobe wall.

"This is the surprise," he said, still in a tone of mystery.

Jana was shocked when they walked up to the front door of the largest building and Fletcher entered without knocking. She half expected this to be some out-of-the-way restaurant and she felt like an intruder as he helped her remove her jacket and led her to the living room. A piñon fire was blazing merrily away in the tiny *hogar* and a bottle of wine and two exquisite crystal glasses were placed on a silver tray next to the fireplace. It was one of the most beautiful rooms she had ever seen.

Fletcher, who had been quietly observing her puzzled reaction, finally spoke. "Welcome to my home, Jana."

"Your home?" Jana's surprise was completely unfeigned. This was certainly the last thing she had expected. "Your home?" she repeated.

"Yes," he said, laughing modestly. "Since you're sharing your home so graciously with me I thought I would return the hospitality."

"But who really lives here?" Jana's dismay was rapidly turning into panic. "Really?"

"Let me tell you the whole story from the beginning. I know that this must come as a shock. But let's have a glass of wine and sit by the fire. I could do with a little warmth after our day in the snow."

Jana allowed him to pour her a glass of wine and seat her near the roaring fire. He paced restlessly about the room, occasionally gesturing with his wineglass to make a point. Jana was struck by his attractiveness, particularly here in his natural setting. His ruggedly handsome features were even more appealing in the dimness of the room, outlined distinctly against the brightness of the fire.

"When I first came to New Mexico I knew that if I was truly going to make it on my own as an artist I would do so in spite of the handicap of wealth, which I had in plenty. As you know, New Mexico already has a greater share than it deserves of wealthy dilettantes. I was determined not to be one of them. When I bought this house one of the conditions of the sale was that the realtor never reveal my identity as the owner. I thought Taos would be the best place in the world to paint. But that was a superficial judgment and I soon discovered that I liked the life in Santa Fe much better. So I kept the house largely as an investment. Periodically the realtor who manages it for me rents it out to tourists and there is a Spanish couple who live here as caretakers. The only person in Santa Fe who even knew of its existence was Lee—and now, of course, you. She and I used to come up here and spend the weekends working. I would be able to paint for hours and she would read and catch up on paperwork. I owed so much to her—and this was a way of repaying her. I haven't been here in several months, not since you came to Santa Fe, in fact. I haven't wanted to come—for obvious reasons. But I thought that you might enjoy it and we could have some privacy for a change. There are no phones here, you see."

Jana followed his explanation with close attention. What were the obvious reasons for his not wanting to leave Santa Fe? Whatever his reasons, he wasn't in Santa Fe now, and quite obviously he expected her to spend the night here with him alone. Realizing this, she felt a surge of anger that after last night he would so quickly assume that she would be willing to repeat the experience. Never had she been so furious! The very fact that Taylor could beckon him to her side with a mere phone call did nothing for Jana's self-esteem. She looked up to find Fletcher gazing intently at her and anger got the better of her.

"You arrogant male chauvinist!" she spouted with true fury. "It's bad enough to play two women off against each other, but to take it as a given that I would be delighted to spend the night here alone with you is unthinkable! You might at least have consulted me first!"

"Now wait a minute!" Fletcher put up a restraining hand. "What's this nonsense about playing two women off against each other?"

"Damn it, Fletcher, don't play the innocent with me!" Jana's anger was so great that she blurted out what had been troubling her all day. "It only took one phone call last night to get you to rush to Taylor's side this morning!"

"Is that what you thought?" Now Fletcher was equally angry. "How dare you assume so much about my behavior? For your information I spent several hours this morning digging both our cars out of snowbanks! For some reason which escapes me now I didn't think it would be a task you'd enjoy undertaking yourself! Perhaps I was mistaken!"

Jana was shamed into silence. Both vehicles had appeared as if by magic this morning. How could she have been so thoughtless? And the thought of Fletcher out there in the freezing cold digging them out alone after his long trek through the snow made her feel truly ashamed. She really didn't know what to say.

"Do you think so little of me? How can you underestimate what happened between us?" Fletcher asked, his voice softer now. "As for the phone call last night, I told you—that was just a neighborly check. In storms like that we all call each other to see that everyone is safe."

"Oh, Fletcher," Jana said. "I *am* sorry. I've been such a fool. How can I ever make it up to you?" She looked up into eyes that were tender and warm with affection.

"I'm sure I'll be able to think of something," he returned, reaching down to touch her lips with the lightest of kisses. Just as Jana's blood began to race through her veins with renewed desire he stood up and smiled down at her. "But first let's enjoy the delicious dinner I've planned for us. For once we have all the time in the world."

Jana rose and followed him through the luxurious house to the kitchen, where she tossed a green salad while he expertly broiled steaks and popped potatoes into a microwave oven. All tension between them gone at last, they laughed and joked in the affectionate manner of lovers. Jana was impressed by the elegance of the house, which was almost austere in its grand simplicity and masculine furnishings. She was reluctant to ask more questions. Fletcher would tell her whatever he wanted her to know when he was ready to talk about it. For the moment she was content to be sharing the evening with him and she too felt for the first time that they had all the time in the world.

After a leisurely dinner in an elegant dining room before still another fireplace Jana and Fletcher did the dishes together and then returned to the living room for a glass of brandy.

Sitting next to Fletcher on a large red pillow, Jana felt a thrill of contentment as his arm went around her shoulders. Looking down into her eyes, Fletcher took her drink from her and placed it beside his on the low table next to the sofa. Then he turned to look her full in the eyes and bent his dark head down to hers to claim her lips in a passionate kiss. Jana, lost in the moment, could do nothing but respond.

After the warm sweet embrace which seemed to last forever Fletcher drew back and looked at Jana with a question in his eyes. "I want you to know, Jana, that I'm not assuming anything—especially after last night. And speaking of last night, I only hope it was as wonderful for you as it was for me. Dear heart, I'm asking—I want you. I want you here with me tonight, in my house, just the two of us. Is that all right? What do you want, darling?" His fingers were playing with the delicate gold chain she wore around her neck and Jana felt as though he were about to undress her. A thrill of sensuous delight raced through her body at the thought of a seductive striptease and she was powerless to fight off the growing spell of excitement.

"Fletcher Logan," Jana said with true seriousness, pausing as if lost in thought, "I want *you!*" And before she had time to marvel at the spontaneity of her response Fletcher's lips were crushed against hers, his tongue searching the inner crevices of her mouth, his hands gripping her shoulders passionately.

Jana moaned beneath the intimacy of his kiss, and as his hands moved down her arms she found herself arching against him, her firm breasts pressed against his chest. Carefully, tenderly, he pulled away from her just enough to slip off her sweater, kissing the sensitive satiny skin above her lacy bra. Without undoing her bra, he eased her breasts above the lacy edge and with his tongue traced tiny circles around the firming nipples.

"Oh, Fletcher," she whispered, running her fingers

through his hair as she twisted against him with hot desire, "I've never felt anything like this before." And she pulled him closer to her, running the tip of her tongue around his ear. Groaning, Fletcher reached up behind her and pulled down several more of the large red cushions from the low sofa. Pushing her back against them, he began to remove the rest of her clothes, and reaching upward, she began to unbutton his shirt, both of them fumbling in their haste to be reunited.

Jana thought that she could be casual about this, that she could take this experience for what it was, simply an affair, a sexual interlude, but she was soon unable to separate physical and emotional responses as she was again swept away by her powerful response to Fletcher's skill as a lover. His mouth dipped to a shoulder, a breast, to the sensitive skin that awaited his true lovemaking, then returned to her mouth again and again, teasing her to even greater heights of desire.

But now she knew this game and she could play it as well as he. She knew what aroused him, from experience now as well as female instinct, and she knew that her effect on him was both powerful and profound. She knew that she was a desired and desirable woman and she gloried in her ability to give pleasure as well as receive it.

Fletcher seemed amazed, totally enthralled. "Woman, what are you doing to me?" he demanded. "Do you know what you're doing?"

"Oh, yes, I do," she assured him. "I just hope that you appreciate it. After all," she added with mock sophistication, "two can play at this game. It *is* more fun that way, don't you think?"

"You she-devil!" he groaned as he forced her back on the pillows, determined to give her some of her own medicine. His kisses were not so gentle now, his passion less restrained than it had been the previous evening. And Jana found herself responding less and less inhibitedly now that she knew her own sensuality. Their bodies were a tangle of heat and moisture and they slid and tumbled around each other, now on the soft cushions, now on the harsher fabric of the rug.

Then there came a moment when both of them knew that this was no longer a game, that the teasing had to stop. And Fletcher, his body arching over hers with a moment's hesitation before making the inevitable connection, looked at her in silence; then, finding the answer in her eyes, he joined his body with hers in a rocketing spiral of sensual fury, both of them straining to make the union even more total, more complete, until finally both of them were spent with the eventual release, which was even more explosive than either one had expected.

Jana collapsed against the pillows, feeling simultaneously depleted and fulfilled. "I thought that would last forever," she breathed, reluctant to break the silence of their sensual stupor.

"That's just the way I want you to feel," Fletcher murmured. "Whatever makes you think that I'm through with you?" he asked.

"Oh, Fletcher, you don't mean . . ." she began, but all too soon it was quite apparent that he did . . .

Later, her head resting on his shoulder as they were

lying with their arms around each other, gazing into the fire, Jana said, "I've never been so happy."

"My darling," he said, "I've only just begun."

And Jana gave herself up to the promise in his voice, hoping that it was really true, choosing for the moment *not* to think beyond this moment, this piece of perfect happiness.

7

·ᵉᵍᵍᵍᵍᵍᵍᵍᵍᵍᵉᵉ·

Jana lingered a moment beside a graceful silver bowl, a present from Lucille Rising Star, the artist she had had an opening for the previous week. She ran her fingers lovingly over its shining surface and marveled at its texture. Lulu, as she liked to be called, had insisted that Jana accept it as a gift.

If Lulu had only known, Jana reflected, that the show was as great a gift for the gallery as it had been for the artist. Jana would never forget that evening—the gallery had sparkled with the beautiful silver works of art and the admiring crowd of patrons had quickly bought up most of the objects. Lulu had been so proud, her tall form standing in the middle of a group of admirers, her black hair, held in place by silver combs, flowing down her back. And Jana had been proud as well—proud of discovering this talented young artist, happy that she could be the dealer to present her to the public.

But she had been more than proud—she had been relieved. The substantial commissions from the sale of Lulu's works would do a good bit to help the gallery's precarious financial situation. She and Tony had spent hours poring over depressing balance sheets, cutting corners wherever possible. They had both been pleased by the financial success of Lulu Rising Star's show, but Jana knew that much remained to be done. She hoped that the opening had been an omen, a sign that the tide was turning in her favor, but it was still too soon to tell.

Her blue eyes softened as she looked around the gallery, checking to be sure that things were in order before she called it a day. The place had become precious to her. It was a little before five, early to be closing, but it had been a long, hard day and she was ready to leave. Besides, her workday today wouldn't end at the gallery itself; she knew that she would be "onstage" that night at Taylor Randall's annual Christmas reception. She didn't relish the thought, but she knew that she had to make a good appearance.

Santa Fe's most prestigious patrons of the arts—the old guard—would be there, as would the many rising young artists who were often as outrageously flamboyant as their wealthy counterparts were decorous. Jana enjoyed the unpredictable mixture of the two groups in the relaxed ambience of Santa Fe. That very mingling was Santa Fe's greatest charm. Jana knew that she herself had yet to win the community's total confidence and that the successful future of the gallery depended on the ease and grace with which she managed to move between the two groups. She put on her full-length camel-colored cashmere coat and wished she could muster some enthusiasm for the evening's plans.

"What time shall I pick you up tonight?" Tony had just finished totaling the day's receipts and was turning off the lights. She had been so absorbed in her own thoughts that she had almost forgotten that he was there with her in the gallery. "Eight-thirty be all right?"

"That would be fine, Tony. Come a few minutes early and I'll give you a drink. I'll look forward to seeing you." She was putting on her fur-lined suede gloves.

"Great. I'll see you then." Suddenly standing beside her, Tony reached out and buttoned the top two buttons on her coat and gently lifted her chin until their eyes met. "A party may be just what the doctor ordered," he said softly, teasing her about the earnest look on her face. "All work and no play . . ."

Jana couldn't help laughing, but she was uncomfortable under his close scrutiny. "All right, you'll see; I'll be the prettiest one there."

"I don't doubt it for a minute." Tony reached to brush a strand of hair from her face and Jana felt herself stiffen ever so slightly. For a moment she was almost afraid that he was fighting the impulse to kiss her good-bye. "See you later," he said instead.

As Tony walked through the door and down the street Jana thought she saw Fletcher's truck pass by, but she wasn't sure. "Men!" she exclaimed to herself. In her heart, she was embarrassed, sensing that Tony's gesture had merely been meant as reassurance, but wondering if Fletcher had really gone by drove all thoughts of the other man from her mind. As they had all day, her thoughts drifted back to the arrogant Mr. Logan. The harder she tried not to think of him the more the memories flooded her mind and it was only with the greatest difficulty that she managed to concentrate on anything else at all.

Tony honked at her as he drove past the gallery, startling her from her reverie. She waved back at him from the front door, where she stood, and then turned and locked the door behind her. She was fond of Tony and didn't want to hurt him. She hoped she hadn't accepted his invitation for the party for all the wrong reasons. Maybe she should have gone by herself.

Well, what's done is done, she thought as she climbed into the van. I just have to make the best of it.

She turned on the heater and sat for a few minutes, waiting for it to warm up. In spite of her good intentions she was having a hard time shaking the despondent mood that had plagued her ever since that morning.

The day had started under a thick covering of dark clouds and it had been hard to take the weatherman at his word. But by noon, as promised, the sun had pushed away the threat of snow and the afternoon had glittered with brightness. Without the blanket of clouds, though, the temperature had dropped.

Jana loved the cold weather and wished her spirits would brighten as the day had. She had been relieved that morning when Tony offered to escort her to the party, had told herself that it wouldn't matter, that she and Fletcher were good friends, business associates who had had a wild fling, nothing more.

Good sense guarantees nothing, she grudgingly admitted as she headed home. As far as she was concerned she and Fletcher still had a lot to learn about one another. Things had been going too fast. Too much was being taken for granted. She needed some time to evaluate her feelings for him and had no intention of committing herself to a serious relationship on the basis of sexual attraction alone.

Although she knew in her heart that she loved him she wasn't at all sure that he felt anything other than physical attraction for her. She had a job to do, one that required all her energy. The gallery was important to her, and until it was firmly on its feet it would have to come first. Fletcher, of course, had no way of knowing just how serious the situation there really was.

When she and Fletcher had returned from Taos Jana had had a hard time putting her feelings into words. For the second time she had allowed treacherous desire to lead her into his bed. So much for good sense! But good sense had nothing to do with it. She wanted him—she had said as much—but even more than that she wanted to be his equal. And she felt that she wouldn't be until she had firmly established herself within the community and knew that the gallery was financially secure. But living in the same house made it so hard! She was always conscious of the fact that he was just beyond the connecting door and she fought to maintain control, to return the relationship to what it had been during her early days in Santa Fe.

Fletcher had stubbornly refused to understand what she so haltingly attempted to express in words. "I can help you," he offered. "I don't really understand what it is that you're driving at, but I can help you if you'll just let me."

Jana shook her head. "I have to do it myself. And if you want to help me you can do it by giving me some time, by letting me work this out for myself." Her determination was shaky at best, but she resolutely refused to be swayed by the longing she felt for him, even then.

"It's bad enough that we share the same house; can't you see? It would be even worse if the whole town suspected that the relationship was more than it is." She knew that this was a cheap shot, for she had never been concerned about other people's opinions before, but it was the only thing she could think of.

Fletcher's anger was cold and swift. He retorted coolly, "But Jana, I thought it was already more than that. You're acting like a small-town girl. This is Santa Fe—nobody cares."

"I do." Jana's voice was quiet.

And with that the discussion was at an end. Fletcher was angry; Jana was determined. There was really nothing more to say. Or was there?

Turning as he left the room, Fletcher had lashed out at her, "Have it your way, then. But don't expect me to wait around for you."

Jana had been hurt and angry but, at least initially, relieved. The pressure was off. Maybe later, he would understand.

The two of them had reverted to the relationship they had originally shared. They met each other occasionally in the house, usually in the kitchen and inevitably under the eyes of Maria, which made it easier. Jana ached with desire for him, but this was the way she had decided she wanted it. "Be careful what you wish for," she said softly to herself. "You might get it."

Jana roused herself from the memory of that painful discussion and noticed that she was almost home. Wearily she went over in her mind the things she needed to do to get ready. The drive to the ranch had in some ways set the world in order for her, though she still smarted with the pain of memory. She allowed herself to relax and enjoy the scenery for the remaining minutes of the drive home. The serene view of the mountains and their stunning majesty always calmed and soothed her. Boston seemed a world away now. She was cheered by the time she reached the house and was actually looking forward to wearing the new dress she had found. Maria would help her. Supper would be ready and everything would be all right.

In spite of herself her good spirits fell when she saw that Fletcher's car was parked in its usual spot. She really didn't want to face him before going to the party, but it looked as if she would have to. There was no hiding from herself the disappointment that she was not going with him, but then, he hadn't asked, probably because he thought she would have refused anyway.

When she entered the kitchen she was dismayed to find Maria getting ready to go home. The older woman was quick to explain. "I'm so sorry, but one of my children is sick; Juanita, the little one. Dinner is ready, of course, and Fletcher said it would be all right for me to leave. I am sorry. But I do have a present for you—in a bag in the refrigerator. I brought it for you to wear to the party. I'll see you tomorrow, if that's all right."

"Of course it's all right. I just hope that Juanita will be all right. We can manage just fine. And thank you for the present. I know I'll love it. You just take care of Juanita and we'll see you when she gets better."

Jana saw Maria off, then turned to face Fletcher, who had hovered in the backgound during this entire conversation. He was smiling at her, motioning her to sit down as he ladled out bowls of soup. "I knew it would be all right with you if Maria left early. She works so hard for us and sometimes it's hard to remember that she has a family of her own."

Jana slipped out of her coat and gloves and sat down, thanking him gratefully for the warm soup he placed before her. "I know what you mean."

They made small talk throughout the simple meal and then rose simultaneously to do the clearing up. "You go ahead and get ready for the party," Fletcher said. "I'll finish this. By the way, what time do you want to leave tonight?"

"What did you say?" Jana stopped halfway through the door, not at all sure that she could believe her ears. She turned to look at him in complete astonishment.

"I said, what time would you like to leave? There's hardly any sense in taking two cars all that way when we live in the same house, is there?" Fletcher laughed down at her. His hands were busy in the soapy water doing dishes and he returned his attention to the task.

Jana was filled with dismay. "But, Fletcher . . . I'm

sorry. Tony offered to take me to the party and I said that would be fine. I didn't think you were interested in taking me. You haven't said a word about it."

"I didn't really think that I needed to," Fletcher said coldly. "I see that I'll have to stand in line in the future."

"Come on, Fletcher," Jana said, thrown off balance by his anger. "It really isn't worth getting upset about."

"I'm not upset," he replied calmly. "But don't you think that this is a pretty silly game you're playing?"

"It's not a game. And it's not silly. I can't imagine why you assumed that I'd be going with you. We really don't know each other well enough for you to be making those kinds of assumptions." Inwardly she was delighted that he *had* assumed they'd go together, but if she were to admit that now she would be too vulnerable.

"We certainly know each other a lot better than we did when you first came here." His meaning was unmistakable.

"Fletcher, let's not go through this again. And especially not now. It's going to be a long evening."

But he wasn't through with her. "Are you in love with him?" he demanded as she was turning to leave the room.

"Of course not."

"Good. He's not your type."

Jana's entire body stiffened with anger. How dare he decide who was and who wasn't her type? "I don't know what makes you think you'd know."

"I know more than you'd like to think I do." And

with this final shot he turned and left the room, slamming the door to his part of the house behind him.

This is not going to be one of my better evenings, she said to herself as she went to her room to get ready. She was sorry that they had parted in anger, but she was angry, too.

A little while later Jana felt her self-confidence return as she gazed at herself in the mirror. The new dress, the one that she had purchased with such delight, was everything she had thought it would be. Indian in style, the soft layers of turquoise trimmed with elegant silver braid fell about her slender form with grace. Her startling blue eyes, gazing back at her from her mirror, reflected the pleased look of a woman who knows that she looks her best.

Elegant silver sandals, a little impractical for the weather, completed the effect. Surely it was worth it to be a little cold. Jana's fingers trembled as she fastened a beautiful necklace of silver and turquoise about her neck. It was perfect with the dress. She felt that she looked every bit the Santa Fe gallery owner and she was filled with determination to shine that evening. She really wanted to be accepted by this group—she wanted to look as if she knew what she was doing. Then and only then could she really begin to have the sort of relationship she wanted with Fletcher. If only he knew how much she wanted to be close to him. But she knew that any crack in the facade could lead to total surrender. It was all or nothing right now, and she had to give her *all* to the gallery, which left little or nothing for Fletcher. This was not the way she wanted it to be forever, but for the moment, it was all she could manage.

She went to the kitchen to take a bottle of wine out of the refrigerator. She had forgotten about the present Maria had mentioned until she opened the door and saw the beautiful pink flower lying there in its plastic bag. She was touched by Maria's thoughtfulness. Impulsively she pinned the flower in her hair behind one ear. Pleased with the effect, she stood back to admire herself. She looked like a gypsy queen. If only Fletcher could see her! But he would. Her heart raced for a moment. She hadn't heard a peep out of his side of the house. Perhaps he was so angry that he had already left, but she hadn't heard the car. These thoughts were soon driven from her mind by the ringing of the doorbell. Tony had arrived; the evening was about to begin.

"Come in, come in." Jana was cordial as she met Tony at the door. "Come in and have some wine by the fire. You'll just have time to get warm before we have to go out in the cold again."

"Cold is not the word for it," Tony said as he entered the house and shrugged off his coat. He usually seemed so casual at the gallery, but tonight, in his tux, he looked quite elegant and attractive.

"I see you kept your promise," he added as he rewarded her with an appreciative grin.

"What's that?" she asked as she hung his coat up.

"You promised that you'd be the prettiest one at the party. And you certainly will be," he added as he continued to take in every detail of her appearance. "The flower is lovely—you'll be the belle of the ball."

Jana flushed with pleasure and led him into the living room, where she poured glasses of wine for both of them. Standing next to her in front of the fire, he raised his glass in a toast. "To you—and to a lovely evening!"

"I'll drink to that." Jana was in the midst of responding when they were interrupted by the sound of someone clearing his throat in the doorway behind them. Jana wheeled about almost guiltily to face Fletcher and gasped.

He looked magnificent in full evening dress. His black and white elegance stunned her into silence.

"Hello, Fletcher," Tony said quickly with his customary good humor. "Jana and I were just having a little drink before the party. Won't you join us?"

"No, thanks," said Fletcher shortly, his eyes never leaving Jana. "It looks like I'm interrupting. I thought I'd go along to the party a little early. There are a few things I wanted to talk to Taylor about and I thought I might have a moment alone with her."

"Well, have a good time. We'll see you there," Jana said sweetly, though inwardly her heart sank at the thought of a private talk between Fletcher and Taylor. What could he possibly say to her? But she knew that she had no right to question his actions—not now.

"Thanks. I'm sure you will." Turning as he left the room, he added, "You look lovely, Jana." His voice was thick.

"Thank you."

There was a brief silence after Fletcher had gone.

"Is there some problem?" Tony asked gently.

"What do you mean?" Jana asked as she compelled herself to resume her hostess manner. "Nothing's wrong. I just don't think that Fletcher's in a very good mood. He can be so gruff at times.''

"If you say so." Tony returned to his wine.

They drank their wine and discussed the house and the things Jana had done to it and their talk was just turning to the gallery when both of them noticed that it was almost nine.

"I guess we'd better leave," Jana said with outward reluctance. The last half hour with Tony had seemed like an eternity and she hoped her feigned cheerfulness had kept him from realizing it.

"You're right." Tony's reluctance was obviously quite genuine. "These parties of Taylor's are often command performances. But the people are nice and the food is generally outstanding. Though how anyone will be able to think about food with you in the room is beyond me."

"Why thank you, gallant escort," Jana said with attempted lightness.

By the time they reached Taylor's house Tony had explained that the party was an annual tradition, that everyone who was anyone would be there, and had told Jana whom she might expect to meet. He promised to introduce her to a few prominent residents she had not so far encountered.

Immediately upon entering Taylor's house, Jana felt a thrill of excitement. Much as she disliked the other woman, there could surely be no more elegant a setting for a party than this beautiful home. It was sparsely but elegantly furnished, so that the coziness of Jana's own home would have looked like clutter compared to it. And Taylor's art collection certainly lived up to its reputation. Jana feigned professional interest in the art, grateful that Tony was with her to fetch her drinks and food and introduce her to the new people. But after a few minutes of party chitchat she found her eyes scanning the room for Fletcher, whom she had not seen since her arrival.

She met and talked with dozens of people, gratified that so many of them had complimentary things to say about the gallery. She was glad to see that Taylor had invited Lulu Rising Star, who rushed across the room to speak to Jana. The two women had a short, pleasant conversation, but then Tony insisted on reclaiming Jana's attention, saying that he had some people for her to meet.

Jana sensed that Taylor was coming to talk to them just as she felt John Peckham's light touch on her arm.

"Jana, you do look lovely," the critic said. "I'm glad you're here. Isn't this exciting? Taylor has finally decided—"

But the rest of his words were lost as Taylor interrupted their conversation. "Jana, welcome to my home. I hope that John hasn't been talking your ear off—I did want this to be a surprise for everyone."

Jana was puzzled, but quickly recovered in time to compliment Taylor on her appearance and the party.

"But you haven't even seen the rest of the house. Here, let me freshen your drink and I'll give you a tour myself. I don't really trust John to do it. He's been talking entirely too much—he'll spoil the surprise."

Jana allowed Taylor to take her arm and lead her to the bar. After Jana had been supplied with a fresh glass of wine Taylor led her into the private part of the house. Taylor, of course, was the perfect hostess.

"Jana, I can't think why we haven't done this

before. I've been longing to show you my collection and lately I've noticed that you have some lovely things in the gallery that might fit in here. We have to get together and talk soon, all right?"

Jana was shocked by Taylor's sudden friendliness. Perhaps she had never given Taylor a chance to be her friend. As they toured the house Jana became engrossed in the art collection. Finally they reached Taylor's bedroom, an elegant black and silver affair. Jana seated herself on the quilted black silk coverlet as Taylor checked her makeup in the mirror attached to her black lacquered dressing table.

"I usually don't enjoy this party very much," Taylor confessed as she put the finishing touches on her appearance. "But this year I think it's going to be special. This is the night I've dreamed of—the night I announce my engagement!"

Jana was shocked into momentary silence, but her good manners rescued her. "Why, Taylor, that's . . . wonderful—I hope you'll be very happy," she said, hoping that she sounded sincere. So *that* was what Fletcher had needed to talk to Taylor about!

"We'll announce it at midnight. I do hope you'll stay." Taylor, satisfied with her appearance, finally rose to return to the party.

"I'll try," Jana said, "though I do have a bit of a headache. It's all this cold weather," she added apologetically.

"Of course." Taylor was solicitous and offered aspirin.

"I really do think I'll get Tony to run me home," Jana said. "But again, I hope that you'll be happy."

"I'm sure we will," Taylor said, "and thank you.

Now I'd better go back and apologize for interrupting John. He'll be angry at not having had much chance to talk to you."

Jana was grateful for some time alone. She looked at herself in Taylor's mirror, all joy gone from the evening. Her new dress suddenly seemed dowdy and the flower that she had pinned in her hair looked suddenly garish and silly. Compared to Taylor she looked as if she was dressed for a high school prom. She unpinned the flower and left it on the table.

Her desolation was complete. She had lost Fletcher. By insisting on having things her own way, she had driven him right into Taylor's arms. It was all due to her foolish pride. But perhaps this was as it was meant to be. Taylor and Fletcher obviously belonged together. They were two elegant creatures, at home in a world of art and money where Jana would never feel comfortable, never be anything but an outsider. Jana would just have to accept things as they were. And she had to admit that the way things were was largely her own fault. She had insisted on putting her professional life first; it looked as if that was all she would be left with. But what was it worth if it had cost her Fletcher? The thought that she would never again share his embrace was almost more than she could bear and knowing that she had brought it on herself only made it worse. The fictional headache had become a painful reality; her temples were now throbbing in earnest.

She couldn't hide in this room forever. Pulling herself together, she returned to the party, where she found Tony waiting with her coat and evening bag. He rushed to her side.

"I was so worried about you," he said, helping her

into her coat. "Taylor told me that you weren't feeling well, so I gathered up all your things and was looking for you. Shall I take you home?"

"Yes, thank you," Jana said, grateful for his dependable concern. As he opened the door for her she stole one more glance at the party. Her eyes were drawn to Fletcher—he was standing in a group with Taylor and John Peckham, laughing and talking as if he hadn't a care in the world. And, of course, he didn't. He was about to announce his engagement to a woman he obviously loved. Jana was out of his life forever.

Tony, out of deference to her headache, was silent most of the way home. When he reached the door of the ranch he merely kissed her lightly on the cheek and said, "I'll call you tomorrow. Take care of yourself; get some rest."

"Thanks, Tony," she said in a small voice. "You go back to the party and have a good time. I'm sorry I wasn't a better companion."

"You were just fine," he said in a husky voice. "Just fine." He turned and went swiftly back to his car.

Jana locked the door behind her. Now that she was truly alone she felt as if the emotions inside her would cause her to burst. She went to her room and took off the dress, which now seemed so foolish, and put on her sensibly warm velour bathrobe. She returned to the living room and put some more wood on the fire, thinking that she would sit there until she felt better. She poured herself a glass of wine, sank back in the comfortable sofa and gave herself over to her misery. Looking at a small clock on a nearby table she saw that it was almost midnight. Fletcher would be publicly declaring his love for Taylor and her heart ached as if it would break. She had no idea how long she sat there, blaming herself, hating herself, for the mess she had made of their relationship.

She was about to pour herself another glass of wine when she heard a noise from the kitchen.

"It's probably nothing," she told herself despite the thrill of fear that ran through her. As she heard footsteps coming down the hall toward her she became absolutely paralyzed.

"Well, *you* came home early," growled the last voice she had expected to hear that evening. Fletcher!

"I might say the same for you," she shot back in surprise. "I didn't expect to see you at all tonight."

"Obviously," he said drily, his voice low with carefully controlled anger. "Perhaps that's why you thought this would be an ideal time for a rendezvous with Tony. But I *do* live here."

He approached her threateningly and she shrank back into her corner of the sofa. "It's hardly your business what I do, especially considering the circumstances." Before she knew it he was next to her.

"Oh, you think not?" he growled. He took the glass of wine from her hand and placed it on the table. Swiftly he took her in his arms, his mouth coming down on hers in a hard, punishing kiss. This was not a kiss of passion—it was a kiss of anger.

Despite herself Jana was about to respond when she was filled with shame, shame for all of them— herself, Taylor, Fletcher. What was he thinking of? He should be with Taylor at this very moment! She struggled against him and finally succeeded in pushing him away, though his face remained frighteningly close to hers.

"Can your Tony Phillips give you that?" he muttered with controlled anger. "Can he?"

"Oh, Fletcher, no," Jana said quietly, and at the words he was kissing her again, this time in the way she loved and knew so well. Against all her wishes she could feel every womanly instinct in her rise up to meet the passion of his kiss. But somewhere inside herself she knew that the situation was wrong—sick and hopeless. If only she could control the desire she felt for him . . . If only . . . If only she had never met him, never fallen in love with him. And now she had lost him forever.

After the long, seductive kiss came to an end Jana found that tears were coursing down her flushed face. Somehow she found the courage to say what she knew she must, "Fletcher, this is all wrong. You don't love me. Why do you persist in punishing me this way?"

Fletcher drew back as if she had struck him, his face tight and controlled. "Jana," he said with icy calm, "you're making a terrible mistake." Without hesitation he left the room.

8

Channeling her anger and grief into a more productive direction than she had taken the night before, Jana threw herself into her work the next morning, hoping against hope to get her mind off Fletcher and his engagement to Taylor. She was at the gallery early—more than two hours before it would be open to the public—sweeping the highly waxed hardwood floors and dusting the glass display cases with a vengeance that shocked even her.

She had dressed meticulously in a forest-green wraparound skirt with soft suede boots and a yellow cashmere cardigan over a pale yellow silk blouse. She had pulled her hair back with silver combs made by Lulu Rising Star, who had also designed and made the silver and turquoise bracelets she wore. The two delicate bracelets jingled against each other as she dusted and she was all too aware of the incongruity between her clothes and the menial task she had so welcomed this morning. She was determined to do anything and everything to get her mind off Fletcher and his outrageous behavior.

The least he could have done was tell me himself, Jana thought bitterly, which he still hasn't done! She was hurt and angry that Fletcher hadn't had the courage to tell her that he and Taylor planned to be married. Instead he hid in the corners and let Taylor break the news to her. He was a heartless coward! Jana had to laugh in spite of herself. If she really believed all this of Fletcher, why did she still care so much?

Catching a glimpse of herself in the glass showcase she had been dusting, Jana saw that the careful makeup she had applied this morning didn't completely camouflage the agony she felt inside. There was, to the discerning eye, a hint of the tears shed in the privacy of her bedroom.

What's your problem anyway? What's with you? she angrily and impatiently demanded of herself. Being so completely in love with the wrong man was a totally new experience for her and learning to deal with it a miserable task.

Time to grow up, face facts. Life is no bowl of cherries. Jana was whistling in the dark with such stern lectures to herself and she knew it. She knew it would take time—a very long time.

Today the gallery seemed like a refuge for her now that the rest of her life had fallen apart and she was glad, for it still filled her with excitement and energy.

She didn't know what she would do without the gallery and loved being there by herself, working late or coming in early as she had this morning. The hours she put in at the gallery had increased significantly as she had attempted to withdraw from Fletcher's desire for a deeper relationship. The very silence of the rooms spoke to her and she thought of the peacefulness she found here as the real legacy from her aunt.

This particular morning the gallery's quiet seemed especially comforting. She couldn't help wondering if Lee Grayson had spent these same long hours alone here, if she too had found solace in the hard work entailed in keeping the gallery a sound business enterprise. It was hard for Jana to imagine the sophisticated and beautiful Lee Grayson, who had been described to her, ever walking this same painful path, but she remembered the story of Lee's running away from home to this strange and impressive country with the artist she had been forbidden to see. No one knew what had become of that young artist and Jana thought after all that perhaps Lee too had known what it was like to be scorned by a lover. Maybe they had more in common than Jana realized and she hoped with all her heart that Lee had been spared the humiliation she had suffered the night before when she learned the truth, not from the man she loved, but from his fiancée.

Imagining that she shared more with Lee than a love of art was small comfort for Jana who, having finished the sweeping and dusting, began the end-of-year inventory. She was glad that it was late December; she needed a job that required all her concentration. And it would be good to have the inventory out of the way before she began work in earnest on Fletcher's opening New Year's Eve.

She got out a clipboard and the proper forms and sharpened several pencils. One way or another she would bridle her unpredictable emotions and keep her mind off Fletcher—once and for all!

At ten o'clock, when she pulled up the shades and unlocked the front door, she had been so engrossed in her work that the brightness of the clear, sunny day came as a real shock to her. She might as well have been in another world. Her mind had finally been given a much-needed respite from the turmoil that had nearly exhausted her and she was beginning to think she had things under control, for a while at least. After a wistful look at the midmorning plaza teeming with seemingly carefree tourists and a few familiar shopkeepers on errands she returned to her clipboard and her work.

Thirty minutes later she was making a pot of fresh coffee in the tiny kitchen and thinking over the sale she had just made when she heard the front doorbell.

Looks like it's going to be a busy day, she thought happily to herself as she poured a cup of hot coffee and headed back toward the main room. At least *something* was going well. Walking through the archway which separated the main room from the two smaller rooms, she felt herself instinctively stiffen at the sight of Taylor, arm in arm with John Peckham, coming through the door. John was carrying what appeared to be a box of doughnuts and sweet rolls from the pastry shop down the street.

Jana hadn't expected to see the two of them this morning—especially together!—and she didn't relish the thought of making small talk. But before she had time to decide how to best handle what seemed to her an awkward situation Taylor rushed forward, her face filled with genuine concern.

"There you are! We've been so worried about you ever since you left the party! We missed you—everyone asked about you." Taylor, looking absolutely radiant in a bright red jump suit and a sporty mink jacket, put her arm around Jana and gave her a little hug. "You certainly *look* as if you're better."

"She certainly does. In fact, that's quite an understatement, if I do say so myself." John was pulling up one of the brightly colored director's chairs, motioning for Jana to sit down by the front counter. "You sit here and take it easy. We can't have the prettiest and most knowledgeable art dealer in town getting sick on us again. I'm beginning to think Fletcher knows what he's talking about when he says you work too hard."

At the mention of Fletcher Jana bristled and was about to deny that she was overworked. But Taylor, without giving her a chance to protest, said quite genuinely, "He certainly does. All it takes is a glance around this place to know that someone is putting in far too much overtime."

John pulled up another chair and Taylor sat down beside Jana. "O.K. We're listening. What have you got to say for yourself? If you're still feeling bad you shouldn't be here at all."

Jana was speechless. The two of them had descended upon her so unexpectedly and with such obvious high spirits—both talking at the same time and making such a fuss over her—that she hadn't had a chance to get a word in edgewise. She had been taken completely by surprise. And the greatest surprise of all was Taylor's concern—it was without a doubt genuine.

Jana finally found her voice and said, "I'm much better. Really I am."

"We've been really worried about you. You looked so pale last night." Taylor was sincere; there was no mistaking it.

"Beautiful but pale," John added gallantly.

"I'm so sorry. It was a wonderful party. I wish I had been able to stay longer," Jana said, getting up from her chair. "But look at me, sitting here, letting you spoil me like this. I'm fine, really I am. Let me get you some coffee. I just made a fresh pot."

"That would be great," John said enthusiastically. "Just the thing to go with these sweet rolls." He wasn't paying much attention to the pastries, however, because he was walking around the front part of the gallery, looking at the painting on the easel by the front window.

"That's wonderful, don't you think?" Jana said, referring to the painting John was admiring. "I bought it last week from an artist who lives alone up in a little cabin in the mountains. He was something of a character and seemed pleased that I liked his work." She turned to go in the kitchen, relieved to have a moment or two alone to gather her thoughts.

She was flustered and hoped she didn't sound as confused as she felt. What on earth was Taylor doing with John Peckham?

Maybe it's not me that's crazy after all, she thought

to herself as she poured two mugs of coffee. Maybe it's this crazy place. She would have expected any woman who had just announced her engagement to be with the man she was going to marry. However, conventional propriety seemed to be a thing unheard of in Santa Fe.

What business was it of hers anyway? Taylor and Fletcher were both adults with lives of their own. Being engaged didn't automatically mean a person had to give up other friends or a former way of life. In spite of herself Jana flinched at the pang of jealousy that stabbed through her. She had to admit to herself, even if somewhat grudgingly, that Taylor had what Jana wanted more than anything else in the world—a full and complete life all her own that depended on no one—the very thing she had so desperately tried, a few weeks before, to put into words for Fletcher when she told him she needed more time.

It was no wonder Fletcher found Taylor so irresistible. What man wouldn't? Jana thought, pulling herself up sharply from her daydreaming. She put the sugar and cream on a tray with the coffee and some napkins and spoons. She was determined to be a gracious hostess. After all, this was her gallery and she had a responsibility to fulfill.

When she walked back out front John was standing with his arm around Taylor and they were smiling at each other. If Jana hadn't known better she would have sworn that they had just kissed. Now she knew she was letting her imagination run wild.

"Oh, here she is. We've found a painting we both like." Taylor looked up when Jana entered the room.

"Don't you think that's a good omen? We had hoped we could find ourselves an early wedding present while we were over here checking on you."

"A wedding present!" Jana was flabbergasted, but did her best not to let it show.

"Well, maybe it is too early to call it a wedding present," Taylor said, reacting to the surprise in Jana's voice. "Maybe we should call it an engagement present." Taylor turned to John and kissed him on the cheek.

Jana was dumbfounded. Suddenly all the pieces fit; it all made sense. She quickly recovered from her surprise and said with what she truly hoped was graciousness, "I don't know what I could have been thinking of! I completely forgot to congratulate the two of you. You must be very happy."

"We certainly are," John said without taking his eyes off Taylor.

"Speaking of happy," Taylor said to Jana, taking a cup of coffee, "you've certainly made all the difference in Fletcher. He's apparently been doing some good work from what I hear and last night was the first time in ages we've seen him in one of his black moods. He was really despondent after Lee's death. We all tried to cheer him up, but nothing worked. He's been a different man since you came to Santa Fe, though. I think seeing the gallery run so expertly again has been part of it."

Taylor set down her cup and looked directly at Jana. "But that's not all—something else has made the real difference. I couldn't help noticing that you were both having a difficult time last night. Please don't think I'm

141

trying to pry into something that's none of my business, but if there's anything we can do to help, you will let us know, won't you?"

"I had no idea. . . . I don't know what . . ." Jana was blushing; she literally didn't know what to say.

John, as if sensing from the look on Jana's face that they had hit on a sensitive matter, swiftly changed the subject, saying brightly, "Do you think you could have this painting delivered to my home tomorrow afternoon, Jana dear?"

"Oh, yes, of course." Jana shot him a grateful glance. "That will be no trouble at all."

Both she and Taylor followed his lead after that and the three of them chatted amicably while Jana finished writing out the receipt and making the necessary arrangements. As John and Taylor were getting ready to leave Jana impulsively kissed Taylor's cheek with real affection.

"I really do appreciate your thoughtfulness this morning. It's meant a great deal to me." Jana found that she couldn't help liking Taylor in spite of their differences these past months.

Taylor smiled and said, "I hope we're going to be good friends."

"So do I." Jana meant what she said. She felt, as she watched them walk down the street, as if she and Taylor had been circling each other warily since her arrival in Santa Fe, each trying to decide what to make of the other. She was glad she had such positive feelings now and realized just how lonely she sometimes was.

Jana breezed through the rest of the day as if a great weight had been lifted from her shoulders. She knew she and Fletcher still had a lot to discuss, but she couldn't help feeling that at least they now had a chance to discover each other anew.

At four-thirty Jana slipped back into the kitchen, shutting the door behind her. It had been a hectic afternoon, all things considered, and she wanted to freshen up a bit before she called it a day. She brushed her hair, looking in the full-length mirror on the back of the kitchen door. The pale yellow blouse brought out the golden highlights of her hair and, unbuttoned at the neck to reveal just a suggestion of the softness of her breasts, was alluring.

Resisting the impulse to close early, she did some last-minute straightening and, at five o'clock sharp, locked up the gallery. She dashed down the street to a florist shop and bought some mistletoe she had seen in the window that morning. The florist insisted on tying a red ribbon around the stems of the green bouquet and Jana thought that it was a lovely touch.

She didn't want to go home empty-handed that night. If she and Fletcher were going to have a chance to start over she wanted to get off on the right foot. And she knew that, whatever else eventually happened between the two of them, she owed him an apology.

The ride through the mountains from Santa Fe to the ranch was, as always, soothing to her. A magnificent sun was setting and she was reminded of that first sunset she and Fletcher had shared so many months ago. That's one thing that doesn't change around here, she thought.

By the time she drove up the driveway she was feeling calmer and more at peace with herself than she had felt in a long time. For the first time she was looking forward to Christmas and she was already planning ahead to the gifts she wanted to buy. She was going to have fun choosing a wedding present for Taylor and John.

Fletcher's truck was already parked in the garage and Jana felt harsh reality closing in on her, putting a damper on her giddiness. She realized that seeing Fletcher again after last night's fight was going to be more difficult than she had thought. She was glad he was home, but some part of her dreaded the initial confrontation. He might not be willing or able to forgive her behavior, even when he knew the real reason behind it. And leaving the party with Tony in such a hurry had certainly not been the act of a sophisticated woman. How was she ever going to explain all this to Fletcher? Then she was struck with the thought that she might not have a chance to explain. He might not care one way or the other. Well, there's only one way to find out, she thought to herself as she got out of the van.

This is no time for false pride, she thought as she opened the front door. The delightful and unexpected aroma of popcorn, of all things, met her as she entered the house and from the front entrance she could hear Fletcher whistling "Jingle Bells." He obviously hadn't heard her come in and she stood for a minute at the doorway to the living room, watching him unobserved.

He had bought a beautiful blue spruce and was concentrating intently on hanging a string of popcorn on the tree. She saw what seemed like hundreds of tiny lights blinking off and on, making the whole room look like something out of a fairy tale. The fire was going in the fireplace and there were two wineglasses sitting on a silver tray next to the red pillows and the hearth.

Fletcher had on a turtleneck and a pair of blue jeans. There was no doubt about the power she saw in the determined set of his jaw and she was aware of the sensual effect he had on her—even at this distance she had to catch her breath against the sweet desire that flowed through her body.

She thought that he was the most incredibly beautiful man she had ever known and all thoughts of caution were left behind. She noticed that Fletcher was eating as much popcorn as he was stringing for the tree and she had to smile.

"Aren't you afraid you're going to ruin your supper with all that popcorn?" she asked from the doorway. Her heart was racing and she hoped her voice sounded natural.

He turned toward her, putting another handful of popcorn in his mouth. His silver eyes were sparkling with fun and he laughed. "Are you kidding? At the rate I'm going I may not even want breakfast." His impish grin gave him an engaging boyish look that Jana found irresistible.

"Looks like fun. May I help?" Her blue eyes met his without wavering.

"Who do you think is going to do the cranberries?" he teased her gently.

Jana was holding the mistletoe behind her back. She decided that this was as good a time as any to surprise him with it. From across the room she threw the bouquet of mistletoe to him.

"Here, catch!" she called without moving from the doorway.

"Ho, ho, ho! A regular Santa Claus she is! What tree did you climb for this?" he joked, quite obviously delighted with the present.

"The highest one, of course. And I'd swim the widest stream, too," she added earnestly.

Fletcher grinned at her and the two of them stood looking at each other as if neither wanted to break the spell of enchantment that had fallen over them. Jana didn't understand the sudden change in his attitude, but she was grateful for it.

After a moment Fletcher said in a soft voice, "May I have this dance?" He bowed gallantly, holding out his hand, the bouquet of mistletoe in front of him.

"I'd be delighted," she said, walking across the room and into his arms. As they began waltzing she looked up into his eyes and could tell that he had been genuinely touched.

"Don't you think we could use some music?" she asked, following his lead around the room.

"My heart is singing so loudly I don't think I'd be able to hear over it. Can't you hear it?" he smiled down at her.

"As a matter of fact, I think I can, now that you mention it." She smiled back up at him as he led her by the twinkling lights of the Christmas tree.

Fletcher stopped in front of the fireplace, sat down on the hearth and pulled Jana down beside him.

"Hi," he said.

"Hi, yourself."

"I don't really need this, do I?" Fletcher tossed the

mistletoe to one side, pulling Jana close. Their lips met gently at first and then with real passion. Jana felt herself giving in to him completely, her hands caressing the back of his neck. She moaned with pleasure as his tongue, hot with desire, sought hers. Crushing her in his powerful arms, he pulled her closer and she felt his cheek next to hers.

"No, you don't need anything," Jana whispered, running her hand through his dark hair, teasing his ear with the tip of her tongue.

Fletcher held her at arm's length and said, "Jana, I'm sorry about last night. I shouldn't . . ."

Jana looked at him in astonishment. "You're sorry? Fletcher, what on earth for? I was an absolute idiot—running out of the party like that, thinking you were engaged to Taylor."

"Is that what you thought? Whatever gave you that idea?" Fletcher had both hands on her shoulders and smoothed down her sweater, rubbing her arms beneath the silk.

"Hold me close," she whispered and shuddered with her need for him.

"Oh, darling, of course." Fletcher held her against his strong chest and caressed her hair as she rested against him. "What's wrong, darling? Why are you upset?"

"I've been such a fool. I should have known better. It actually embarrasses me that I was so jealous of another woman." Jana sighed and smoothed her hands over his back, aware of the strength that lay in his muscles.

"You have no reason to be jealous of anyone, my

ENCHANTED DESERT

love. Not now, not ever," Fletcher promised. "I was jealous last night, too."

"*You* were jealous." Jana sat up with a start and looked at him with amazement. "What on earth for?"

"I was jealous of Tony," he admitted sheepishly. "Well, what was I supposed to think—coming home and finding you in your dressing gown? You're an enticing woman under any circumstances, you know. And that dressing gown is hard to resist." He played with the combs in her hair.

"Oh, Fletcher. I can't believe it. Poor Tony. You know, he didn't even ask me what was wrong. He brought me home without asking a single question. I certainly must have been less than irresistible last night, what with the mood I was in. I imagine he was glad to get rid of me." Jana was perfectly contented sitting there by the fire, Fletcher's arm around her, her head resting on his shoulder. She had no trouble talking to him this time.

"He's a good friend, all right. He came over this morning after you left. Boy, were you a ball of fire! Up and out of here before I had my first cup of coffee."

"What do you mean Tony came over *here?*" Jana could scarcely believe what she was hearing. Tony had come back to this house?

"You bet he did. Gave me a piece of his mind too, in no uncertain terms. I didn't know what he was all riled up about at first. Apparently he misunderstood Taylor too. He let me have it for leading you on, said he'd personally wring my neck if you got hurt again. And he was mad enough to do it too." Fletcher drew her close and she felt the warm strength of his arms.

"Tony told me something else, too," Fletcher continued in a subdued tone. "Jana, why didn't you tell me how concerned you were about the gallery's financial problems?"

"I just couldn't," she said quietly. "I was going to—today, in fact—but before now I just couldn't. It would have made our relationship so much more complicated than it already was—and it would have hurt my pride so terribly to admit my fear of failure. I see now that I was mistaken and I'm terribly sorry. It was bad enough that Tony had to know." She relaxed into the comfort of the strong arm encircling her shoulders.

"Well, I hope you're not angry with Tony for telling me. I practically had to pry it out of him. It just made me so *angry* to imagine him knowing what was really bothering you when I didn't." Fletcher's voice was slightly angry, but there was a tenderness there, too. "Jana, why did you really feel you had to keep it from me? I want us to have a relationship where we share everything—work and love, joys and problems. Don't shut me out ever again."

They were both silent for a long moment, thinking of how the pain of the last weeks could have been avoided. Finally Jana looked up at him and kissed him gently, determined to lighten the mood of seriousness which had suddenly descended upon both of them.

"You know what I think? I think maybe we have a lot of good friends," Jana said, laughing quietly. She told him about Taylor's visit to the gallery.

"Sounds like Taylor's doing some matchmaking," Fletcher said and his smile clutched at Jana's heart.

"Tony's doing his share of nosing in where he shouldn't too," Jana said with mock resignation.

"I don't think we're going to need any more help, do you?" Fletcher murmured gently, looking deeply into Jana's eyes.

"I think we're going to be able to manage this on our own—for a while at least." Jana was content—as content as she had ever been in her life.

Fletcher moved his arms around her again and this time there was a great urgency in his kiss. She felt a rising heat flood through her veins as she returned his desire with her own. His hand traced a line from her throat to her breast and he bent over to kiss the sensitive bare skin above her lacy bra. Jana arched her back against his arm and beneath his hand her nipple hardened. Her eyes were closed against the waves of desire, but she could almost feel his sigh of regret.

"If we're going to get this Christmas tree decorated tonight I think we'd better do it now, while I still have my wits about me. I don't think we should leave it undecorated, do you?" Fletcher pinched her nose playfully and stood up, pulling her up beside him.

She laughed at his obvious reluctance. "Our first Christmas tree," she said with mock seriousness. "Don't you think we ought to drink to that?"

"I completely forgot the wine. I guess my mind was on better things," Fletcher teased lightly as he opened the wine and poured a glass for her.

"Now let's see how good you are with a needle and thread." He laughed, handing her a bowl of fresh cranberries.

"I bet you think I don't know how," Jana teased back, tossing a cranberry at him. "But don't think I'm going to let you have all that popcorn without a fight. I'm starving."

When they had finished decorating the tree they stood back admiring their handiwork. Jana had tied red velvet bows and put them on the tree with the cranberries and popcorn. Fletcher had hung garlands of silver tinsel when he finished with the popcorn.

"It's the most beautiful tree I've ever seen," Jana said. She turned to Fletcher and said, "I never thought I could be so happy."

"What happened to starving?" Fletcher laughed. "Let's go see what we can find in the kitchen. You don't think Maria forgot about us, do you?"

"Not a chance," Jana replied, rallying after her moment of nostalgia. She gladly followed him to the kitchen, where they discovered a huge pot of Maria's stew—one of her best dishes. Jana baked cornbread while Fletcher made a salad and set the table. They laughed and talked all through supper, discovering that in spite of nibbling popcorn they still had healthy appetites.

While cleaning up the kitchen Fletcher told Jana about how well his latest paintings were going. "I haven't painted like this since before Lee died. The last few weeks, in fact, may have produced my best work." He was pleased and Jana was delighted that he had shared something so important with her.

When they returned to the living room Jana's thoughts returned to the gallery and the work that lay ahead if the opening of Fletcher's new show was to be the success she intended.

Fletcher noticed Jana's solemn mood, and as if he could read her mind, he said as he put his arms around her, "Oh, no you don't. Not now. The gallery will have to wait. Tonight it's my turn. I want you all to myself—if, of course, you don't already have plans."

He looked down at Jana, who was staring into the blazing fire, as if she were contemplating his proposal. "Well, yes. I think that could be arranged," she said, "but on one condition."

"Anything, my love." Fletcher searched her eyes, trying to decide what Jana's condition might be.

"Let's take the phone off the hook," Jana said sheepishly.

Fletcher threw back his head and roared with laughter. "I beat you to it, my friend. I took it off the hook before dinner."

9

Jana awoke at first light, scarcely able to believe where she was until she saw Fletcher's curly dark head asleep on the pillow beside her. She looked at him for a long moment, savoring the pleasure of being able to observe him at rest, and her eyes lingered lovingly on every feature. After last night's lovemaking she felt so close to him, felt that she knew every part of him as he knew every part of her, and she blushed with pleasure at the memory of her own uninhibited behavior. She was just admiring Fletcher's heavily lashed eyes when she noticed that his firm mouth was trembling slightly, as if he was suppressing a smile.

"Oh, you," she muttered. "Playing possum, were you? Well, you can just play by yourself. I'm getting up." She moved quickly to the edge of the bed.

"Not so fast!" came the deep growl and any thought of escape was quickly dashed as he grabbed her around the waist and pulled her back down beside him which, Jana reflected to herself, was a very nice place to be. He nuzzled her neck and shoulder, planting a string of kisses along the sensitive skin there, the warmth of his lips contrasting with the rough texture of his morning-whiskered face. "I'm not at all ready for you to get up. Judging from the light outside, it's early yet. Plenty of time for what I have in mind."

"And just what do you have in mind?" Jana laughed, certain that she already knew the answer.

Their mutual amusement quickly changed to passion. Their playful caresses turned again to sensual delight as they began again the intimate voyage of the night before. Jana was amazed at her own body—Fletcher seemed to know exactly what brought her the most pleasure as he skillfully, swiftly enticed her to the brink of ecstasy with his subtle, creative caresses. Something ancient and powerful awoke in her as she responded to his secret invitation. Their bodies joined in tender combat as she yearned toward him, returning kiss for kiss, pressure for pressure, intimate touch for intimate touch.

Fletcher's sensitive artist's fingers traced lazy erotic circles around her breasts, his lips and tongue finishing what his fingers had begun as he recorded her, tasted her. She drank in his affection as if it were a heady nectar and she was soon intoxicated with the feast of smells, tastes and textures that his body presented for her delectation. She had never been so aware of a man, from the rough stubble of his jaw to the powerful muscles of his thighs as he settled his long form over hers, renewing once again the intimate bonds of love they had begun to forge with one another. Jana took his weight eagerly, straining against his naked body as he once again took full possession of her.

They looked deeply into each other's eyes as they made love and both were pleased to see the passion and desire reflected there. Jana pressed the muscles of Fletcher's back, clutching convulsively as he brought her to new heights of erotic magic as if she wanted to bind him to her forever. And Fletcher was tenderly unrelenting as his claim on her deepened. By now their bodies knew each other's rhythms and they teased and encouraged each other along the path of passion as they journeyed to that place beyond time or memory. Finally Jana felt her whole being shudder in excitement and she exploded with pleasure at the exquisite torment of contact, gasping with her release. Fletcher followed her there, his hoarse groan of relief changing to a smile of sensual wonder.

They basked in the warm afterglow of their love-making, unable to keep from touching each other. "Now aren't you glad I didn't let you get up?" Fletcher teased gruffly, one finger tracing the outline of her sensitive, now almost bruised lips.

"At this rate I may never get up." She laughed throatily, a contented laugh of sensual delight.

"That suits me fine," he growled and he began to touch her again, his intentions obvious.

"No, no," she protested, disentangling herself from his embrace and racing from his bedroom to her own bathroom.

She was reluctant to leave his bed so quickly, equally reluctant to wash away the traces of their lovemaking under the shower. She would have liked to bask in the warmth of their togetherness, but it was difficult enough as it was to rouse herself from the stupor of erotic languor. She was rinsing shampoo from her hair when she spied Fletcher's tall dark form through the shower curtain.

He pulled aside the curtain and stepped in beside her. "No sense wasting water," he said matter-of-factly, and taking the soap, he began to soap her entire body vigorously. Jana laughed, admitting that she was trapped, and she soon began to writhe and twist under his tender ministrations as he covered her body with creamy foam, exploring every inch of her slender form. She opened like a flower under his insistent touch and the soap proved a delicious adjunct to their lovemaking as she began to stroke Fletcher's back, raking her nails through the soapy lather. He responded by teasing the inside of her slender thighs and both of them were soon lost in a frenzy of renewed desire. Jana had not thought such delight possible.

Finally, all passion spent, they emerged from the shower and toweled each other dry with exquisite roughness. "Look at us." Jana laughed, seeing their reflections in the mirror. "Aren't we absurd?"

"I don't think so," Fletcher replied with mock offense. "I think that you're quite lovely—and that I'm quite lucky." Jana rewarded him with a brilliant smile and a hasty tender kiss before racing off to her room to dress.

As she finished up with her makeup she could hear Maria rattling around the kitchen, making preparations for breakfast. She hoped Fletcher was safely back in his part of the house. She had grown to care a great deal for Maria and she certainly didn't want to shock her. Going in for breakfast, she greeted the older woman with a smile and a cheery hello and sat down with a cup of coffee. A few minutes later Fletcher joined them in the sunny room.

"My, my," Jana said, taking pleasure in teasing him. "Look what the cat dragged in!"

"We can't all be morning people," Fletcher retorted with a teasing glance of his own. "I have to conserve my strength for my busy evenings!"

Jana blushed and was momentarily silent. Then the two of them broke into shared laughter, stopping only when Maria cast a questioning glance in their direction.

All too soon breakfast was over and Jana was ready to leave for the gallery. She had a challenging day ahead, the most important item on her agenda being a meeting with Tony to go over the month's receipts for the gallery and evaluate its overall financial picture. Even though she would have preferred to spend the day with Fletcher she knew that her mind would be on the gallery. It was a responsibility that she took very seriously and today would be an important day for her. For one thing, she hoped that they would see some last-minute Christmas shoppers and she was looking forward to the bustling activity. But more importantly, she was curious to see what Tony would say to her. She had a puzzling feeling of foreboding, but she rapidly pushed it to the back of her mind and summoned up a cheery mood to face the day ahead.

Fletcher reached for her as she stood to leave the room. "Wait a second, will you? I'm almost ready to leave myself."

Jana groaned for Maria's benefit, but in her heart she knew she would wait for Fletcher anytime. Her heart leaped at the sight of him, ruggedly handsome in casual clothes, and she smiled at the memory of how ruggedly handsome he remained without them.

The two of them said good-bye to Maria and tramped out into the cold and brilliant day, laughing and talking. Fletcher walked Jana over to the van and opened the door for her, smiling up at her after she had climbed in. "I'll follow you into town—perhaps I could drop by with some lunch?"

"That would be lovely!" Jana smiled back. "And now that I know your taste in women is as good as your taste in food I'll leave the choice completely up to you!"

"I'd much rather have you for lunch than food," Fletcher shot back quickly, "but given that this is such a busy time of year I guess I really have no choice."

"That's right, you don't," Jana retorted, "but it will be nice to see you for lunch anyway. And pick something up for Tony as well, will you? It should take us awhile to go over all the receipts and he may still be there by lunchtime."

"Well, it does go against all my male instincts to feed a man I thought was my rival, but I suppose I can be a graceful winner." This was said in a mock-grudging tone.

Unable to resist a mischievous impulse, Jana reached down to shut the car door. "Don't get too cocky, my friend. You haven't won yet!" And she quickly started up the engine and began to back out of the driveway. Fletcher, left standing there, could only shake his fist at her in mock dismay, but Jana was sure she saw him dissolve into laughter as he turned to go toward his truck.

Jana's heart was singing as she drove into town. She turned on the radio and sang along with real enjoyment. Suddenly her life seemed to be falling into place. Now, if only Tony has some good news for her . . . She steadfastly refused to dwell on any possible problems, determined to hang on to her Christmas spirit, a feeling of joy and satisfaction that she knew stemmed as much from her new understanding with Fletcher as it did from the holiday season. She looked around at the gorgeous little town of Santa Fe as if she were seeing it for the first time. Who would ever have dreamed that a bookseller from Boston would have found such happiness as an art dealer in the great Southwest? No wonder New Mexico was called the Land of Enchantment!

She was still humming Christmas carols to herself as she maneuvered the van into her parking space behind the gallery. As she walked around to the front door she was struck again by the sight of the plaza all dressed up for Christmas. The streets and storefronts were decorated with greenery and most of the roofs were lined with luminaria, small paper bags weighted with sand and containing candles, which would be lit in the evening to make the whole town look romantic. Could any place in the world be more beautiful?

She unlocked the front door, feeling again a rush of pride as she looked around the elegant expanse of the gallery, so much of it now truly her own creation. She hoped that somewhere her unknown aunt Lee Grayson was proud of her. She had tried so hard to make the gallery a success, but only Tony could tell her if her endeavors had been effective.

By the time Jana had walked through the gallery to

the office she had already shrugged off her coat and gloves and was mentally preparing herself for the day ahead. Then she went back to the tiny kitchen and put a pot of coffee on to perk. She liked the smell herself and found that gallery customers, especially in this cold weather, would often linger when tempted with a cup of freshly made coffee. Besides, Jana felt that she and Tony would probably need it before their session was over.

She walked around the front room, making sure that everything was in order. There wasn't a dusty frame or objet d'art in the place. Everything positively gleamed with love and care. As it should, Jana thought to herself, because I do love it.

Glancing at her watch, she noticed that it was now almost eleven o'clock; Tony was due any time. Eager to have this crucial meeting begin, she went to the front door of the gallery to see if she could see him coming down the street. No sign of him yet, but she enjoyed seeing the little town outside the windows come to life. Most of the shops that lined the street were now open and a few tourists were beginning to make their desultory way through the business district. Ah, there was Tony!

The bookkeeper entered the gallery, shivering with the cold. "Good morning, Jana," he said brightly, though his face wore a worried look. She held his briefcase for him and helped him off with his coat; then he removed his gloves and rubbed his hands together for warmth. They walked through the gallery to the back office, exchanging pleasantries on the appearance of the gallery, the weather, the number of people on the streets, until Jana thought that she would fairly scream with tension. But Tony was not to be rushed.

Only after he was seated at Jana's desk with all of his papers and calculator spread out in front of him did he take his first sip of the coffee Jana had gotten for him. She had taken a chair near the office door so that she could keep an eye on the front of the gallery, but in reality her attention was focused strictly on what Tony had to say to her.

An hour later the bad news was really beginning to sink in. By now the desktop was littered with papers and Tony had rolled up the sleeves of his sweater and was calculating furiously. Jana, who had been interrupted periodically by browsers and occasional purchasers, was sitting again in the chair across from him, her features marked by an unaccustomed look of despair. This morning had seemed so bright and hopeful. And she knew that the sales were up, especially after Lucille Rising Star's successful show. How could this be happening? She had worked so hard!

Tony, sensing that she was near tears, was quick to attempt to comfort her. "Now, Jana, I know that the profit-and-loss sheet looks pretty grim and, of course, that's a good reason to be depressed. But every business has periods like this and the best way to get through them is to approach the situation with a positive outlook. What can be done? What is it possible for this gallery to do to pull itself out of such a slump?"

Jana knew that he was right and her fighting spirit slowly began to reassert itself. When she raised her eyes to Tony, the old light of combat and desire to succeed was in them again.

"O.K., Tony, what are the measures we can take to halt our losses? How do we turn this place around?"

Tony looked relieved to hear the tone of challenge in her voice. "Well, in the first place, a truly major successful opening would help. Grayson Gallery needs that right now. The reviews, the attention—all are free advertising, in a sense. I know that we have Fletcher's opening coming up a week from tomorrow. That should do it. I've assembled a few names to add to your mailing list, a few of the wealthy snowbirds who only descend on Santa Fe during the holiday season, people you haven't met yet who might be helpful. And then—and I'm not suggesting this as an immediate measure, but rather as something to mull over—you might consider taking on a partner."

"I was going to suggest the same thing myself," a deep voice behind them said quietly. Jana jumped with surprise. How had Fletcher managed to enter the gallery without her even realizing it? She and Tony must have been lost in their conversation. Turning to him, attempting to summon up a cheery smile for his benefit, she saw that his arms were full of bags from a nearby take-out restaurant.

"Why, Fletcher," she said, "let me help you with the food. And, Tony, I think that we both could do with a break."

Tony swept aside part of the huge stack of papers to make room for the food, while Jana went back to the kitchen for dishes and silver and glasses. When she returned the two men were talking together in low tones, though they seemed to be friendly enough.

"I've brought your favorite lunch, Jana," Fletcher

said in a hearty voice. "Black bean soup and hot buttered *tortillas*. I hope that that's all right with you too, Tony?"

"You bet!"

There was a lull as the three of them munched their *tortillas* and sipped the wonderful soup in silence. Jana was grateful for Fletcher's thoughtfulness, and as they were clearing away the cups and spoons talk again returned to the financial state of the gallery.

Fletcher spoke with calm authority. "You would have no way of knowing this, Jana, and I hesitate to mention it because of the timing, but Lee and I often discussed my buying into the gallery. If you're in need of help I would be delighted to be an investor or a partner, whichever you prefer. It would be strictly a business arrangement, of course."

"That *is* true, Jana. I was present once when Lee and Fletcher discussed it, but your aunt was a rugged individualist who preferred to stick it out alone," Tony quickly added.

After a moment's silence, during which she looked at the two men who were gazing at her so expectantly, hoping that she would take this easy way out, Jana spoke quietly. "And so am I. Thank you very much for your generous offer, Fletcher, and don't think for a minute that I don't appreciate it. But this is something I have to do myself for the memory of Lee Grayson and for me, too. You have to understand that, especially after our talk last night. I have to succeed or fail by my own efforts."

Tony sighed, looking from Fletcher to Jana. "Well, if that's the way you want it, Jana, I'll do my very best to help you. But if I were you I'd certainly keep Fletcher's offer in mind. Will you?"

"Of course," Jana replied with an attempt at brightness and a dazzling smile for Fletcher's benefit, "but I think that the most important thing Fletcher can do for us right now is to get back to his painting so that this opening next week will be the very best we've ever had."

Fletcher rose to his feet and came to stand next to her, looking down into her eyes with warm affection. "What the boss says goes, Tony. And, Jana, I won't let you down. This *will* be the best opening you've ever had. I promise you that. So right now I'm going out to the ranch to finish a few things up. We'll hang the show after Christmas and usher in the New Year with the most fabulous party—and the most magnificent opening—that Santa Fe has ever seen." He bent to kiss her cheek and then he was gone.

Jana was grateful for the quick kiss, but even more grateful that he left her in privacy to discuss her problems with Tony. She knew in her heart that Fletcher only wanted to help, that he had the money and would be more than happy to use it for her benefit, but then she would never be truly happy with herself; then she would never know if she could have made it in Santa Fe on her own. No, she would just have to tough this one out by herself. She hadn't come all this way to begin a new life only to have it slip through her fingers so quickly.

The next afternoon found Jana still preoccupied with gallery problems, even though it was Christmas Eve. She had spent most of the morning cooking a turkey for the Christmas Eve feast that she would share with Fletcher and then she had retreated to her desk to do the extra invitations for the people on Tony's list. She was also studying the gallery's profit-and-loss statement. So absorbed was she that she was startled by a sudden burst of color from behind her and she turned to see Fletcher plugging in the lights of the Christmas tree.

"So—you're making a list and checking it twice, are you?" Fletcher smiled into her eyes.

Jana laughed for the first time in what seemed like days. "You might say that." Struck by the expression of concern in his eyes she realized that she had been thoughtless to stay so wrapped up in her own problems on the first day of a holiday that she and Fletcher had planned to enjoy together. She also noticed with amazement that it was growing dark outside. Glancing at her watch, she felt even more guilty. "Oh, dear, the turkey—it should be done by now!"

"Relax," Fletcher said with amusement. "You were so busy that I checked it myself a few minutes ago and even to my untrained eye it looked fine. I think everything else is in perfect readiness too. Maria wouldn't leave this morning until she was sure we were all taken care of for the holidays."

"I know," Jana agreed. "It was so thoughtful of her to come in at all today, especially when she has her own family to worry about."

"Well, you're pretty thoughtful yourself," Fletcher replied. "That was a pretty generous Christmas bonus that you gave her and I know she was touched by the lovely sweater."

"She does so much for us," Jana said. "I knew that the money would come in handy for the kids, but I did want her to have something for herself."

"You're a very thoughtful lady," he said, coming closer to give her a light kiss on the lips. "But considering how thoughtful you were to Maria this morning, I would think that you could take a little time off and spend it with me. You light the fire and sit by the Christmas tree and I'll be right back."

Jana, stung by the thought that she had been neglecting him, rose to light the fire. She realized that she was glad of the change—she needed a break. She was admiring the fire and the lights on the tree when Fletcher returned with a bottle of pink champagne and two glasses.

"Let the festivities begin!" he exclaimed ceremoniously.

Jana laughed as he wrestled with the wire and foil wrapper on the bottle. Finally they were rewarded with a loud pop! and Fletcher poured two glasses of the bubbly wine and came to sit next to her.

"And now," he announced, "we'll open our presents!"

"But it's only Christmas Eve," Jana protested. "Don't you want to wait until tomorrow morning?"

"Not really," he replied with an attempt at nonchalance. "I always like to sleep late on Christmas morning. And besides, I can't wait for you to have your present. Just pretend that we're two small children whose parents have just told them that they don't *have* to wait until morning!"

Jana couldn't help laughing at his display of boyish spirits. She thought about her present for him, which had been under the tree for days, and hoped he liked it. "Well, all right," she drawled after pretending to consider the idea. "But on one condition—you have to open my presents to you first."

"Now *that's* a condition I can live with!" He laughed. "Where are they?"

"As if you didn't know!" Jana went over to the tree and pulled out two packages, one large and flat and the other a small box. "I've seen you snooping around under the tree like a six-year-old!" She walked over to him and presented him with the two elegantly wrapped boxes. "Merry Christmas, Fletcher!"

"Merry Christmas, Jana," he replied softly and his voice was filled with emotion as he gazed down at the two presents in his lap. "Which should I open first?"

"Take your pick," she replied. "Though I personally would recommend the larger one," she added, breathing a silent prayer that he would approve of her choices.

Fletcher picked up the large flat package and carefully began to unwrap it, gently removing the tape with his fingers so as not to tear the beautiful gold paper. "Oh, Jana," he breathed softly as he almost reverently lifted up a beautiful art book of Georgia O'Keeffe prints. "I've wanted this. How did you know?"

She was pleased that he so obviously enjoyed it. "I remember the day we were driving to Taos and you talked about her. I'm glad you like it."

"Like it? I love it!" He rose to kiss her tenderly.

"Now, now," she said teasingly, disentangling herself from his embrace with a real effort. "You still have one present left to open."

"Right, right," he said, though he stood there for

another long moment, gazing at her with a peculiar intensity.

"So open it!" she urged, momentarily uncomfortable under the pressure of his gaze. "Here it is," she said, placing it in his hands.

"You really shouldn't have," he said as he began another slow and careful unwrapping. "The book was more than enough."

"I'm just glad you hadn't already bought it for yourself."

"Oh, no," he said. "Paint I'll buy, and paper and canvas, but books are a real luxury that I allow myself only occasionally."

Jana laughed. "Well, it's nice to be able to provide you with a luxury, even if it's just a small one." She watched his face intently as he opened the small box.

"How beautiful—what beautiful craftsmanship," he said with awe as he examined the intricately hammered silver belt buckle. "And, Jana, it's even personalized—my own initials . . . you must have planned this ages ago!"

"Not really," she demurred, pretending modesty, though inside she was incredibly happy that he took pleasure in gifts. "Lulu made it for you. I pointed out that it would be a splendid advertisement for her if you wore it around town and told people that she had made it."

"You bet I will! But first I'll tell everybody who gave it to me! That's the most wonderful part." Jana turned aside from the look of admiration in his eyes.

"Now it's your turn," he continued, "and I want you to sit right there on the sofa by the fire and I'll get your present." Jana returned to her seat and Fletcher walked over to the tree and pulled out a large gift box wrapped in silver foil with blue ribbon. He presented it to her with a little flourish, sitting beside her and reaching out to refill her champagne glass as she began to unwrap it.

"But it's so big! What could it be?"

"Well, you certainly shouldn't act so surprised at its size," he teased her. "I've seen you looking under the tree when you thought I wasn't watching." Jana felt her face flush, but she was so happy that she didn't really care. She did wonder what was in the large box, though; it seemed to weigh very little.

"Oh, Fletcher." She laughed as the first box opened to reveal another smaller wrapped box within. "This is the oldest trick in the book, you know."

"I know," he quipped, "but that certainly doesn't lessen the suspense one bit. Now you'll just have to open the next one."

Which she did, only to find still another small box! "Now really," she scolded him.

"Honestly, this is the last one," he said as she opened the box to find a small blue velvet case, which could only be from a jeweler's. She was curious and felt a mounting anticipation as she gingerly opened the tiny blue case to reveal an exquisite diamond solitaire in a flawless setting. It was simply beautiful.

"Oh, Fletcher," she breathed in a tone of pleasure tinged with sadness. "It's so lovely, the most beautiful ring I've ever seen, but I can't possibly accept it."

"I don't see why not. It's just your size. I want to marry you, darling. The ring means exactly what you think it means."

Jana looked up to see that his eyes were filled with

hope, waiting for her answer. "I'm touched and deeply honored that you want me for your wife. And I want to accept it, but not right now, not until I can work things out for myself and be sure that the gallery is all right so I can meet you on an equal footing." Jana was sorely tempted by her desire to give in to her love for him and become his wife, but it would be too easy to marry Fletcher and let him solve all her problems. She relished her hard-won independence too much to let it go right now.

"All right, my darling," he said in a voice filled with his love for her. "I'll wait for you as long as it takes. But do try to hurry it up a little, will you?"

She stood and kissed him gently, drawing back to say, "Merry Christmas, darling. And good night." It was with a terrible effort that she left him there and went to her own bedroom, shutting the door behind her. She couldn't risk even one look back; she knew that if the expression on his face was anything at all the way she imagined it would be, she would turn and rush to his side and all would be lost.

Some day soon, she comforted herself as she slipped into her lonely bed. Some day soon we can be together and it will be perfect. And the promise was made to herself as well as to the man waiting for her with such love and tenderness.

10

It was New Year's Eve, the day of Fletcher's opening, and as Jana opened the door to the gallery she felt a thrill of excitement and anticipation—her first *major* opening and her first party in Santa Fe! She had put on her favorite apricot-colored wool pants with a matching sweater. Her silky hair was pulled back to one side with a silver comb. Realizing that she had a busy day ahead, she had taken special pains this morning when she dressed. She wanted to look her best all day and knew she probably wouldn't have time even to powder her nose.

A ray of sunlight shot through the door and settled on the beautiful silver bowl that she admired so much. A good omen, Jana thought to herself. This should be a day filled with good omens just like that one. She went about the business of turning on the lights as usual, even though the gallery was closed to the public today. Setting up for such a gala event took a lot of time and effort.

The morning flew by almost without Jana's realizing it. Even at the last minute there was still so much to be done. She spoke to the caterers, who assured her that the champagne and hors d'oeuvres would be ready on time. Next came a phone call to the florist to check on the flowers. Jana had ordered a few arrangements —one for the gallery counter, and one for the refreshments table, unsure whether a champagne fountain would have been festive enough. Trusting her instincts, she stuck to flowers and greenery that were native to New Mexico, thinking that they would best blend in with both the décor and the contents of the gallery. The florists assured her that they would be at the gallery within the hour, so Jana got off the phone and began to rearrange things to her satisfaction.

She was filled with pleasure as she moved about the room, dusting picture frames or pottery that appeared to need attention. But no matter how much she tried her gaze kept returning again and again to Fletcher's magnificent paintings. She and Fletcher had had such a good time hanging the show the afternoon before. Maria had come in from the ranch to help and Tony Phillips had dropped by to lend a helping hand. The four of them had spent an enjoyable afternoon hanging and rehanging the paintings to Fletcher and Jana's satisfaction.

Jana was grateful that Fletcher had given so much thought to the show, for she was reluctant to make suggestions about the placement of the paintings. But she did make a few, and when they were quickly accepted she began to feel comfortable with her role as director. Fletcher seemed to enjoy her comments and to be especially pleased that she liked the paintings, for until he brought them to the gallery she had seen none of them. He preferred to work in solitude and he had denied her access to the studio, saying that she would make him self-conscious. Jana had understood his need for privacy, seeing it as somewhat similar to her own struggle for independence.

The paintings were all that Jana had hoped they would be and even Tony had been awed by the appearance of the gallery once they lined its walls. And looking over the price list that Jana and Fletcher had drawn up together, he let out a long, low whistle.

"Well, I can tell you one thing," he had finally admitted after making a few mental calculations, "if you sell out even *most* of this show your financial problems are over. I think that what we have here is an opening that's destined for success."

Jana, filled with relief, had leaned over to give his arm a friendly squeeze. "I guess that means you'll be there?"

"You bet I will!"

"And it's a good thing too," Fletcher interjected. "I know that I'll be as nervous as a cat and Jana certainly will be too, what with all the things that she'll have to take care of. We really will need one cool head among us!"

"I can promise you that." Tony's voice was firm and the two men looked at each other with obvious respect.

As she worked around the gallery Jana's thoughts kept returning to the previous afternoon. It had been so perfect, so filled with hope. Even Maria had enjoyed the day; despite being occupied with cleaning she had seemed to enjoy being in the gallery with the other three. She had promised to be present at the opening, even though Jana knew that she was a little nervous too. Jana had promised to bring Maria into town with her, for she planned to go back to the ranch to dress and grab a bite of dinner.

Jana felt sure that the opening would be a success— if only everyone would come. Tony had told her that he had heard through the grapevine that people had received their invitations and were excited—both about seeing Fletcher's new work and about coming to the gallery for a gala event.

Just then Jana heard the bell over the door and went out front, hoping that the florists and caterers had arrived. She was determined to do everything humanly possible to make this opening a success.

The young man from the florist carried in two arrangements of flowers. "Those are beautiful," Jana said, showing him where to leave things.

"Just what the doctor ordered."

Jana moved the receipt book and other loose papers from the counter so he could put one arrangement there. The other had gone on the refreshment table. She watched him with interest as he looked around the gallery at the paintings. She hadn't yet had any reaction from someone outside her immediate circle and she waited, holding her breath, wondering how he would like Fletcher's latest work.

"Looks like you're going to have some party," the young man said as he walked around the room, looking closely at the paintings.

Jana didn't say anything. She wanted to give him time.

"Boy, these are something else!" He was visibly impressed. Jana could feel herself relax as he stood in front of one of the most beautiful landscapes.

"Who is this artist, anyway?" He turned to Jana, who wondered if her face revealed the apprehension she felt inside.

"Fletcher Logan. He's one of our most talented artists." She hoped she sounded nonchalant.

"I've never seen anything before that I wanted to take home with me right away to hang in my living room. But I sure could live with one of these." The young man was obviously affected by what he saw. "I'm working part-time before school starts again. But someday I'm going to be able to buy one of those." He moved to the front door, about to leave.

"We'd love to have you come back tonight for the opening. Fletcher will be here. You can meet him." Jana wanted him to feel welcome anytime. She knew he just might be able to afford a fine painting one of these days.

"Gee, thanks. I just might do that. Well, I guess I'd better go. There are a lot of parties in this town tonight."

"Yes. I imagine New Year's Eve is a busy time for a florist. I hope there aren't too many other parties for our guests to attend. I want everybody on our mailing list to come here." Jana had to laugh at her own eagerness as she closed the door behind him. She was delighted to have had such a good first impression and hoped he would come back that night.

Hours later Jana noticed that the afternoon had

almost completely gone. The flowers shone with their own beauty without detracting from the works in the gallery. The champagne was cooling in the kitchen and the refrigerator was loaded with trays of elegant hors d'oeuvres, ready to be placed on the table at the last minute. Everything glowed with a festive air and Jana was thrilled as she made one last tour around the gallery.

Of course, the party preparations had given the place a festive air, but the magnificence of Fletcher's paintings outshone everything. Jana was proud that Grayson Gallery would be bringing these works to the attention of the public, and no matter what the financial outcome of the evening she was doubly pleased with the work she had accomplished in the short time she had been in Santa Fe. Now if only lots of people would come tonight! If only they would show her that she had reason to be proud.

Jana drove back to the ranch in a daze. Even though she had plenty of time to have dinner and dress for the party her mind was racing with the few last-minute details that demanded her attention. She hoped that Maria had pressed the aqua dress that she had worn to Taylor's party. During the earlier part of the week she had promised herself that she would buy another dress for the opening, but somehow the time to do so had eluded her. She remembered that Fletcher had told her how pretty she looked that night and she could only hope that he would be proud of her on this occasion as well.

Before she knew it she was marching through the back door to find Maria presiding over the kitchen.

"Ah, you're home!" The older woman smiled.

"Dinner is all ready. You can eat something and then take a long leisurely bath and dress. I'll change while you're bathing and then I'll help you dress, so we'll be there in plenty of time."

Jana appreciated the way Maria had taken charge and she rewarded her with a grateful smile. "Thanks, Maria. Any word from Fletcher?"

"Oh, yes," Maria said with a concerned look on her face. "He left a little while ago. Then a few minutes ago he called from town and said that he'd meet you at the gallery. He took some clothes with him so he could change there. He said to tell you that you really wouldn't want to be around him today and that he was always a wreck right before an opening."

At Jana's quizzical look Maria went on, as if to affirm Fletcher's message, "And he really is, Jana; I've seen him. If he were here he'd do nothing but make us all nervous. It's really better this way. Now eat your dinner and we'll see him later."

Jana had no choice but to obey. Maria had cooked a cheese omelet and made a lovely fruit salad. Jana was grateful for the light supper but, for once, scarcely noticed Maria's good cooking. She was actually relieved that Fletcher was already in town. She appreciated the way he had stayed away from the gallery all day; by not hanging over her, he was showing that he had perfect confidence in her.

Jana allowed herself the luxury of a brief soak in the warm bath Maria had thoughtfully drawn for her. As she relaxed in the scented bubblebath she felt the tension of the day drain away from her. Her whole body tingled with anticipation and she found herself looking forward to the evening. It was New Year's Eve, after all, and what better way to begin her first new year in Santa Fe than with an opening for Fletcher? The evening lay before her, filled with promise, and she would rise to the occasion.

When she reentered the bedroom she saw with gratitude that Maria had placed everything she would need for the evening on her bed. The aqua dress looked perfectly pressed and her shoes, stockings and evening bag were all ready. There was even a single rose in a vase on her dressing table. Maria had thought of everything.

A few moment later Maria's face appeared in her doorway. "Can I help with anything?"

"Please," said Jana, whose fingers were trembling at the clasp of her necklace. "If you could just do this for me I think I'll be ready."

Maria capably fastened the necklace and stood back to admire Jana's reflection. "You look lovely, my dear; your aunt would have been so proud of you."

During the ride into town Jana was grateful for Maria's companionship, for the two women made small talk about everyday things until Jana felt quite calm. So many people have faith in me, Jana thought to herself. I just won't let them down.

As she maneuvered the van into her parking space she glanced at her watch and was relieved to see that she was an hour early. Right on schedule. As they entered the gallery Maria exclaimed at its loveliness and Jana was pleased at the woman's immediate response.

The two women busied themselves with last-minute details, Maria taking charge in her own inimitable way. Before half an hour had passed the trays of hors d'oeuvres were attractively placed on the table and glasses, napkins and champagne were all in readiness. Jana realized that no last-minute disasters had presented themselves. Glancing at her watch, she saw that there were only thirty minutes before the party would begin. Much to her surprise she heard the bell over the door ring and suddenly Fletcher was there.

He was dressed in fawn-colored suede and the honey color of the soft leather only set off his dark magnificence. He looked calm and collected and Jana could find no trace of anxiety in his strong features. She moved forward to meet him.

"Hello, my love," he said lightly, bending to kiss her cheek in spite of Maria hovering about. "Are you all ready for the big night?"

"Of course," Jana replied, attempting to match his calm. "But, you know, it's really your big night, not mine." She looked up into his face and caught her breath at the tender concern in his eyes.

"With you looking the way you do," he replied, his steel gray eyes scanning her slender form, "I would be a fool to try to steal any of your spotlight. I'm quite content to share it with you. Let's just say it's *our* big night."

The words were prophetic. An hour later, glancing around the gallery, Jana was thrilled to see that it was filled with people even though it was New Year's Eve and the evening was still young. Guests stood in animated groups around the gallery. One large group gathered near the buffet table, chatting and snacking. Smaller groups admired Fletcher's paintings and Jana found herself surveying the scene with undisguised pleasure. The people were as beautiful as the gallery.

Everything from furs to blue jeans, glittering diamonds to heavy turquoise, was worn by the guests.

At one point during the evening Tony took her aside for a moment. Luring her away from her conversation he said that he had to tell her something terribly important.

"Jana, I think you've done it," he said excitedly. "I can't believe how many of the paintings have been sold!"

It was, in fact, almost a complete sellout! It was a dream come true. She knew that she had to tell Fletcher; he would be as pleased for her as he would be for himself.

She thanked Tony for all his help and support and the two of them shook hands, congratulating each other on the evening's success. Then Jana went to find Fletcher and Tony returned to mingling with the guests. Fletcher was nowhere in sight. Taylor, in a pencil-thin sheath of emerald silk glistening with gold threads, was standing with John and a dark, distinguished gentleman who Jana knew was a critic from one of the most prominent art magazines. They interrupted their conversation to include Jana.

"Here's the woman responsible for this; she single-handedly put this show together." Taylor introduced Jana to the internationally known critic.

"I've been wanting to meet you," the distinguished-looking man said. "My name is Porter Johnson." He clasped her extended hand in both of his, drawing her away from the crowd.

"I'm familiar with your work, Mr. Johnson." Jana was delighted to meet this man. Having him here at her first major opening was more than she had dared dream possible.

"I hope you'll consider letting me interview you for the magazine." Porter Johnson looked admiringly at her.

"Well, yes, I'd be happy to. But don't you think Fletcher is the person you're looking for?" Jana was flattered and hoped she sounded professional.

"I want to talk to you both. I'll get him later, but I wanted to be sure of you, first." Mr. Johnson beamed enthusiastically at Jana.

"Where is Fletcher, anyway?" Jana's thoughts returned to the artist and she realized that she hadn't seen or talked to him for what felt like forever.

She and Fletcher had exchanged glances across the room, but both had been hopelessly trapped by their respective groups. Fletcher was usually surrounded by art critics, all of whom, uncharacteristically enough, seemed to be enjoying the opening and Jana had been captured by a number of prospective purchasers and well-wishers. But she was shocked not to see him anywhere in evidence. Her heart sank and she realized how empty the room was without him in it.

Her expression must have reflected her dismay for Taylor and John rapidly detached themselves from a group of eager conversationalists and came to her side.

Taylor had purchased two of Fletcher's paintings earlier in the evening, saying that she thought they were his best work to date. John had agreed with her and the two of them were obviously impressed with the opening.

"Now, Jana," Taylor said in a teasing tone, "I suppose you're looking for Fletcher."

"As a matter of fact, I am," Jana replied, trying to keep her voice even. "Do you know where he is?"

"He told us to tell you that he'd be right back and you're not to worry," John hastily interposed, sensing that Jana was truly concerned. "That was about thirty minutes ago. He also told us to keep an eye on you. Not that you need it, of course. This is the best opening I've ever been to here. Not many people could pull off an opening on New Year's Eve, my dear, but you've done it and done it with style."

"Why, thank you," Jana said, genuinely touched. "But I could never have done it without your help—it looks like all of Santa Fe is here."

"We had nothing to do with it," said Taylor. "You completely won the town over at my party and then created an air of mystery by leaving so early. They knew they'd have to come tonight to find out more about you and now they all want to know you better. Jana, face it, you're a sensation."

Jana couldn't think of a single thing to say, so pleased was she with Taylor's compliment. How could she have so misjudged this woman? At any rate, all that misunderstanding was now in the past and her foolish jealousy would no longer keep them from becoming real friends. Just as she was struggling to find the words to express what she felt she noticed that Fletcher had returned and was in the center of the gallery, setting up a veiled painting on an easel.

Jana was so relieved to see him that she hardly noticed what he was doing. Her eyes slipped to his strong hands, which were busy steadying the concealed painting on its perch. Puzzled, she fought her way through the crowd to his side to find out what was going on.

"Fletcher, what are you up to?" she asked suspiciously, even though he greeted her with a grin. "What is this?"

"This, my love, is a New Year's surprise for you. But I'm not quite ready to unveil it yet. It's almost midnight. Why don't we make sure that everyone has some champagne to toast the new year? Then I'll make a little speech and unmask my masterpiece."

Jana had no choice but to comply. She told Tony and Maria that Fletcher was up to something and asked them to make sure that everyone had a drink. The two of them didn't seem at all surprised and circulated through the crowd, making sure that all glasses were filled.

Meanwhile, the veiled painting on the easel had attracted a good deal of attention, though most of those present were too polite to pry. Within a few minutes, sensing that something was in the air, most of the guests had gathered around it. Fletcher was laughing and joking with the crowd. Having filled her champagne glass, Jana made her way to his side, answering the questioning glances of her guests with a puzzled look of her own. She noticed that Tony and Maria had come to stand near her and she was grateful for their support, even though she knew that anything Fletcher did would be in impeccable taste.

Sensing that the time was right, Fletcher held up his hand for silence. Conversation came to a quick halt.

"I know that it's a little unusual for an artist to make a speech at his own opening, but this is one time when

I really must, even though I haven't been formally asked.''

He paused and John Peckham obligingly said, "Speech! Speech!" in humorous tones.

The crowd laughed and Fletcher sent a thankful glance in Peckham's direction before continuing. "I think that this is a special occasion, not only for myself, but for all of us. This is Jana's first New Year's Eve in Santa Fe and the first major opening at Grayson Gallery in much too long a time. So, I have prepared a special surprise for this evening. I now ask you to join me in a toast to my latest painting. Let me hasten to add, at the risk of sounding terribly egotistical, that it's not for the sake of the painting itself, but rather a toast to its remarkable subject. Ladies and gentlemen, I proudly present to you my very latest work!"

Jana gazed at him steadily as he stood to one side of the painting and removed its protective covering. She was prepared for anything except what actually met her eyes as her gaze came to rest on the painting.

For the subject of the painting was Jana herself! There she stood, in the very same beautiful aqua and silver dress that she was wearing now, the only difference being that she was wearing a gorgeous cactus flower in her hair. As the crowd gasped with pleasure everyone raised their glasses in a toast to Jana as Fletcher came to her side.

Then, quietly, the applause began, first just a ripple, then a rumbling torrent, until both Jana and Fletcher seemed to be wrapped in its warmth. Glancing around at the faces of her newfound friends, Jana wondered why she had ever felt any doubt about being accepted in Santa Fe. She had more friends than she had ever thought.

Tactfully enough, no one seemed to notice as Fletcher took her arm and led her out of the gallery into the clear cool night. Walking a little bit down the street from the gallery, he took her arm and turned her to face him.

"Now, Jana, I have something to say to you and I won't be put off this time. Look up at that moon." Obediently Jana's gaze joined his in silent appreciation of the tiny sliver of silver. The moon was waning.

"Do you see that? Soon it will be a new moon, a new year and, I hope, a new life for us. Now, my darling, will you be my wife?" He took from his pocket the ring he had bought for her for Christmas and held it up questioningly.

"Oh, yes, yes!" Jana replied and the answer was in her face and eyes as well as her voice. For now she felt as if they were truly ready for each other, no misunderstandings, no problems between them.

"Oh, Jana!" Fletcher exclaimed and gathered her close in an embrace that threatened to last forever.

Jana felt her body melt against his in a spasm of sweet longing, all the more intense because she knew what pleasures they could share. She gave herself up to his kiss, not caring for a moment that it was New Year's Eve and that they were practically in the middle of a public thoroughfare. Only after they had paused for a moment did Jana notice that people were leaving the gallery, discreetly going down the street in the opposite direction.

"Oh, Fletcher, I should get back."

185

"Nonsense, darling," he insisted as he grabbed her arm and pulled her back to him. "It's well after midnight. It's time for everyone to go home. Besides, Tony and Maria and John and Taylor knew exactly what I was up to and promised that I could spirit you away and they would take care of everything. By the way, I made sure that they knew that the last painting is *not* for sale and belongs to *us*, for our home. And besides, I have plans for the rest of the evening . . . in fact, the rest of the week."

"And what might those be?" Jana asked, though she knew that she would have gone along with anything.

"Well, I thought we'd start by looking for another cactus flower for your hair. I warn you, it may take all night. It might even take days, so I thought we'd start looking right now." Fletcher kissed her gently and brushed her hair from her face as he looked deep into her shining, expectant eyes.

Jana knew that she would join him in this quest as in all others—for her heart belonged to this man in this place. She had truly found an enchanted land at last.

Silhouette Desire

Six new titles are published on the first Friday every month. All are available at your local bookshop or newsagent, so make sure of obtaining your copies by taking note of the following dates:

JUNE 3rd

JULY 1st

AUGUST 5th

SEPTEMBER 2nd

OCTOBER 7th

NOVEMBER 4th

Silhouette Desire

Now Available

Renaissance Man by Stephanie James

Rare book dealer Alina Corey decided to live like the heroine of her favourite Renaissance book. It worked . . . until Jared Troy, a Renaissance scholar, challenged her to leave her storybook world and face a passion as grand as her dreams!

September Morning by Diana Palmer

Blake Hamilton was determined to control Kathryn but keep his heart free. She tried to rebel in the arms of another man, until a furious Blake promised to teach her a lesson she would never forget—plunging them both into a fiery passion.

On Wings Of Night by Constance Conrad

In one wild night of love Cara Williams had abandoned herself to publisher Quinn Alexander. Now she was faced with the prospect of working for him and wondered if she could deny the fulfilment she found in his arms.

Silhouette Desire

Now Available

Passionate Journey by Thea Lovan

In the silver Moroccan moonlight
Phillipa Bentley was swept away by passion for
Raoul Mendoub, who claimed her sweetness
with his plundering kisses. She tried to rebel
but found this dark, enchanted prince had
bewitched her soul.

Enchanted Desert by Suzanne Michelle

Jana Fleming had inherited Santa Fe's most
famous gallery, but she hadn't expected artist
Fletcher Logan to be part of her legacy as well!
Overwhelmed by his touch, Jana knew Fletcher
was her fate and her future.

Past Forgetting by Pamela Lind

Amanda Adams, prim and proper film
goddess, had finally met her match in
Alex Wojyclas, the principal backer of her
latest film. In his arms her icy reserve melted
and she soon found herself giving in to
passion's implacable demands.

Silhouette Desire
Coming Next Month

Reckless Passion by Stephanie James

Dana Bancroft's stockbroker sense
told her that beneath Yale Ransom's well
groomed exterior there lurked a primal force
. . . anxiously waiting to be released.

Yesterday's Dreams by Rita Clay

He said his name was "Mr. Lawrence,"
but Candra Bishop soon discovered the truth:
he was the stable boy she had adored in
her youth and now she was as much in
his power as ever.

Promise Me Tomorrow by Nora Powers

Harris Lilton was a charmer, the kind of
man artist Jessie Hampton despised—yet
couldn't resist. She knew she couldn't trust
him, but in his arms she was heedless of
all but desire.

Silhouette Desire

Coming Next Month

Snow Spirit by Angel Milan

Joda Kerris' passions flared when she
discovered that Egan, the man she had fallen
in love with, was a lawyer hired to sue her
and Keystone Mountain Ski Resort!

Meant To Be by Ann Major

Before she knew he was her boss, ravishing
Leslie Grant abandoned herself to Boone
Dexter for a single passionate night. Now could
she convince him she loved him?

Fires Of Memory by Ashley Summers

Just when she thought he was safely out of her
life, Adam Kendricks, real-estate tycoon,
returned to San Francisco. This time Gia
Flynn clung to one vow: to conquer him
once and for all.

Silhouette Desire

THE MORE SENSUAL
PROVOCATIVE ROMANCE

95p each

13 □ COME BACK
MY LOVE
Pamela Wallace

14 □ BLANKET OF
STARS
Lorraine Valley

15 □ SWEET
BONDAGE
Dorothy Vernon

16 □ DREAM COME
TRUE
Ann Major

17 □ OF PASSION
BORN
Suzanne Simms

18 □ SECOND
HARVEST
Erin Ross

19 □ LOVER IN
PURSUIT
Stephanie James

20 □ KING OF
DIAMONDS
Penny Allison

21 □ LOVE IN THE
CHINA SEA
Judith Baker

22 □ BITTERSWEET
IN BERN
Cheryl Durant

23 □ CONSTANT
STRANGER
Linda Sunshine

24 □ SHARED
MOMENTS
Mary Lynn Baxter

25 □ RENAISSANCE
MAN
Stephanie James

26 □ SEPTEMBER
MORNING
Diana Palmer

27 □ ON WINGS
OF NIGHT
Constance Conrad

28 □ PASSIONATE
JOURNEY
Thea Lovan

29 □ ENCHANTED
DESERT
Suzanne Michelle

30 □ PAST
FORGETTING
Pamela Lind

*All these books are available at your local bookshop or newsagent, or
can be ordered direct from the publisher. Just tick the titles you want and
fill in the form below.*
Prices and availability subject to change without notice.

SILHOUETTE BOOKS, P.O. Box 11, Falmouth, Cornwall.
Please send cheque or postal order, and allow the following for postage
and packing:

U.K. – 45p for one book, plus 20p for the second book, and 14p for
each additional book ordered up to a £1.63 maximum.

B.F.P.O. and EIRE – 45p for the first book, plus 20p for the second
book, and 14p per copy for the next 7 books, 8p per book thereafter.

OTHER OVERSEAS CUSTOMERS – 75p for the first book, plus
21p per copy for each additional book.

Name ....

Address ....

....